Anonymous

Historical and Descriptive Review of the Industries of Austin,

1885

commerce, trade and manufactures - manufacturing advantages, business

and transportation facilities

Anonymous

Historical and Descriptive Review of the Industries of Austin, 1885
commerce, trade and manufactures - manufacturing advantages, business and
transportation facilities

ISBN/EAN: 9783337096441

Printed in Europe, USA, Canada, Australia, Japan

Cover: Foto ©Andreas Hilbeck / pixelio.de

More available books at **www.hansebooks.com**

HISTORICAL AND DESCRIPTIVE REVIEW

OF THE

INDUSTRIES OF AUSTIN,

1885.

Commerce, Trade and Manufactures,

MANUFACTURING ADVANTAGES, BUSINESS AND TRANSPOR-
TATION FACILITIES,

TOGETHER WITH

SKETCHES OF THE REPRESENTATIVE BUSINESS HOUSES

AND

MANUFACTURING ESTABLISHMENTS

IN THE CITY.

AUSTIN, TEXAS,
PUBLISHED BY THE AUTHORS.
1885.

PUBLISHERS' NOTICE.

Much has been said and written during the past decade of years concerning the wonderful resources of Texas, the greatest amount of stress, however, being laid upon its advantages for agriculture and stock-raising. The partiality thus exhibited has evidently had a tendency to obstruct the development, through the influence of capital from abroad, of those equally as important interests coming under the head of commerce and manufactures, and has also, in no small measure, been discouraging to the home efforts in that direction. The resources of the State are of such a broad and comprehensive character, as to demand the fullest recognition of every interest in anywise calculated to contribute to the material prosperity of its people; and it behooves every city and town to place before the public at large a succinct statement of the local advantages possessed for building up trade and industry. The wisdom of such a policy is to be seen in the substantial benefits which have followed, wherever the method has been adopted.

No point within the broad domain of Texas, has more to gain by heralding abroad its advantages for commercial and manufacuring capital, than Austin. The Capital, as well as the most beautiful residence city in the State, it also possesses *every* facility that Nature can provide, and many that artifice has contributed for making it one of the chief industrial centers of Texas. Not only are its advantages of the highest standard and its natural resources inexhaustible in extent, but it presents a field of manifold opportunities for the safe investment of capital, skill, and enterprise, which cannot be duplicated elsewhere, nor are they likely to remain long unimproved.

The enterprising business men of the city are vigorously laboring to develop its latent strength as a commercial and manufacturing center, and it is to further their commendable efforts that this volume is placed before the public.

In compiling it, we have been placed under many obligations for the valuable assistance rendered by the citizens generally, and through Messrs. J. W. Robertson, Mayor of the city; J. L. Driskill, Walter Tips, A. P. Wooldridge, E. T. Eggleston, and Ed. W. Shands, we desire to return our sincere thanks for the appreciative interest that has been manifested in the success of the undertaking. That it will result in securing to the Capital City of Texas, the greatest possible benefits is the earnest hope of

THE PUBLISHERS.

July 1, 1885.

GENERAL INDEX.

A

B

C

D

E

F

G

H

J

K

L

M

N

P

R

S

T

U

V

W

Z

TRADE, COMMERCE AND INDUSTRIES

OF

AUSTIN, TEXAS.

INTRODUCTORY.

Though it is a time honored custom among book-makers to give each volume an introductory chapter, clearly for the purpose of more readily securing it a favorable recognition among the reading public, yet it must be admitted that, however important the influence of such a chapter might *once* have been, it exercises but little or *no* weight in this matter-of-fact age, wherein the readers, as a rule, skip the "introductory" and get at once at the pith of the volume. Such being a fact, generally speaking, it certainly is a superfluous labor to observe the old custom in a work devoted to those interests which more immediately concern the world than all others combined, and to which this country in particular is indebted for its wonderful advancement to the foremost rank among nations, its grand successes and magnificent prosperity. And as the title of this volume plainly indicates its object to be the betterment of the Capital City of the great State of Texas through the further development of its trade, commerce and industries, economy of space urges us to dispense with all unnecessary preliminaries and enter at once upon the task before us.

HISTORICAL.

The independence of the Republic of Texas was declared March 2, 1836, and Houston (which had been established as a town site about the same period) was made the temporary capital. Under the administration of President Lamar, the Congress of the Republic passed an act, January 4, 1839, providing for the election of five commissioners, who were authorized to select a site for the permanent seat of government, between the Trinity and Colorado rivers and above the old San Antonio road, which crossed the Colorado River at the town of Bastrop. The site was to comprise a tract of land not less than one, nor more than four leagues in extent, and was to be selected either out of the public domain, from private donation or by purchase, at a cost not exceeding three dollars per acre. The act also provided for the appointment of an agent for the purpose of laying out 640 acres of the land thus selected, in town lots, and after reserving a sufficient number of the most eligible lots for the capital and other necessary government buildings, to sell one-half the remainder at public auction. The site thus laid out was, under the provisions of the act, to be called the "City of Austin."

The result of the labors of the commissioners thus appointed is best told in the following reproduction of their report:

CITY OF HOUSTON, April 13, A. D. 1839.

To His Excellency Mirabeau B. Lamar, President of the Republic of Texas:

"The commissioners appointed under the act of Congress, dated January, 1839, for locating the permanent site of the seat of government for the Republic, have the honor to report to your Excellency that they have selected the site of the town of Waterloo, on the east bank of the Colorado River, with the lands adjoining, as per the deed of the sheriff of Bastrop County, bearing date March, 1839, and per the relinquishment of Logan Vandever, James Rodgers, G. D. Hancock, J. W. Harrall and Aaron Burleson, by Edward Burleson, all under date of seventh of March, 1839, as the site combining the greatest number of, and the most important advantages to the Republic, by the location of the seat of government thereon, than any other situation which came under their observation within the limits assigned them, and as being, therefore, their choice for the location aforesaid.

We have the honor to represent to your Excellency that we have traversed and critically examined the country on both sides of the Colorado and Brazos Rivers, from the upper San Antonio road to and about the falls, on both those rivers, and that we have not neglected the intermediate country between them, but have examined it more particularly than a due regard to our personal safety did perfectly warrant.

We found the Brazos River more central, perhaps, in reference to actual existing population, and found in it and its tributaries, perhaps, a greater quantity of fertile lands than are to be found on the Colorado, but on the other hand, we were of opinion that the Colorado was more central in respect to territory, and this, in connection with the great desideratums of health, fine water, stone, stone coal, water power, etc., being more abundant and convenient on the Colorado than on the Brazos River, did more than counterbalance the supposed superiority of the lands, as well as the centrality of position in reference to population, possessed by the Brazos River.

In reference to the protection to be afforded to the frontier by the location of the seat of government, a majority of the commissioners are of opinion that that object will be as well attained by the location upon one river as upon the other; being also of opinion that within a very short period of time following the location of the seat of government upon the frontier, the extension of the settlements produced thereby will engender other theories of defense on lands now the homes of the Comanche and the bison.

The site selected by the commissioners is composed of five-thirds of leagues of land and two labors, all adjoining, and having a front upon the Colorado River somewhat exceeding three miles in breadth. It contains seven thousand seven hundred and thirty-five acres of land, and will cost the Republic the sum of twenty-one thousand dollars or thereabouts, one tract not being surveyed. Nearly the whole front is a bluff of from thirty to forty feet elevation, being the termination of a prairie containing perhaps two thousand acres, composed of a chocolate colored sandy loam, intersected by two beautiful streams of permanent and pure water, one of which forms at its debouche into the river a timbered rye bottom of about thirty acres. These rivulets rise at an elevation of from sixty to one hundred feet, on the back part of the site or track, by means of which the contemplated city might, at comparatively small expense, be well watered, in addition to which are several fine bluff springs of pure water on the river at convenient distances from each other.

The site is about two miles distant from, and in full view of, the mountains or breaks of the table lands, which, judging by the eye, are of about three hundred feet elevation. They are of limestone formation, and are covered with live oak and dwarf cedar to their summits. On the site and its immediate vicinity, stone in inexhaustible quantities and great varieties is found almost fashioned by nature for the builder's hands; lime and stone coal abound in the vicinity; timber for ordinary building purposes abounds on the tract, though the timber for building in the immediate neighborhood is not of so fine a character as might be wished, being mostly cottonwood, ash, burr oak, hackberry, post oak and cedar, the last suitable for shingles and small frames.

At the distance of eighteen miles west by south from the site, on Onion Creek, 'a stream affording fine water power,' is a large body of very fine cypress, which is also found at intervals up the river for a distance of forty miles, and together with immense quantities of fine cedar, might readily be floated down the streams, as the falls, two miles above the site, present no obstruction to floats or rafts, being only a descent of about five feet in one hundred and fifty yards, over a smooth bed of limestone formation, very nearly resembling colored marble.

By this route, also, immense quantities of stone coal, building materials, and in a few years agricultural and mineral products for the contemplated city can be obtained, as no rapids save those mentioned occur in the river below the San Saba, nor are they known to exist for a great distance above the junction of that stream with the Colorado.

Opposite the site, at the distance of one mile, Spring Creek and its tributaries afford, perhaps, the greatest and most convenient water power to be found in the Republic. Walnut Creek, distant six miles, and Brushy Creek, distant sixteen miles, both on the east side of the river, afford very considerable water power. Extensive deposits of iron ore, adjudged to be of very superior quality, is found within eight miles of the location.

This section of country is generally well watered, fertile in a high degree, and has every appearance of health and salubrity of climate. The site occupies and will effectually close the pass by which Indians and outlawed Mexicans have for ages past traveled east and west, to and from the Rio Grande to Eastern Texas, and will now force them to pass by the way of Pecan Bayou and San Saba, above the mountains and the sources of the Guadalupe River.

The commissioners confidently anticipate the time when a great thoroughfare shall be established from Santa Fe to our seaports, and another from Red River to Matamoros, which two routes must almost of necessity intersect each other at this point. They look forward to the time when this city shall be the emporium of not only the productions of the rich soil of the San Saba, Pedernales, Hero and Pecan Bayou, but of all the Colorado and Brazos, as also of the produce of the rich mining country known to exist on these streams. They are satisfied that a truly national city could, at no other point within the limits assigned them, be reared up; not that other sections of the country are not equally fertile, but that no other combined so many and such varied advantages and beauties as the one in question. The imagination of even the romantic will not be disappointed on viewing the valley of the Colorado, and the fertile and gracefully undulating woodlands and luxuriant prairies at a distance from it. The most skeptical will not doubt its healthiness, and the citizen's bosom must swell with honest pride when standing in the portico of the capitol of his country he looks abroad upon a region worthy only of being the home of the brave and the free. Standing on the juncture of the routes of Santa Fe and the sea coast, of Red River and Matamoros, looking with the same glance upon the green, romantic mountains and the fertile and widely extended plains of his country—can a feeling of nationality fail to arise in his bosom, or could the fire of patriotism lie dormant under such circumstances?

Fondly hoping that we may not have disappointed the expectations of either our countrymen or your Excellency, we subscribe ourselves your Excellency's most obedient servants,

H. C. HORTON, Chairman,   ISAAC CAMPBELL,
J. W. BURTON,   LOUIS P. COOKE."
WILLIAM MENIFEE,

Immediately upon the reception of the report of the commissioners the President appointed Judge Edwin Waller, the agent—as provided for in the act—who with a corps of surveyors, proceeded to the site selected, and entered vigorously upon the duties required of him. He found the so-called town of Waterloo to consist of but three families, and Montopolis, its ambitious rival, two miles below, composed of two families. The first sale of lots was made August 1, 1839, three hundred and six being sold at prices ranging from $120 to $2,800 each, and bringing, in the aggregate, the sum of $182,588. Before the sale, however, the city had commenced rapidly to fill up with good, staunch and hardy citizens, and by the time it took place, many houses had been erected, by parties who were willing thus to build and risk their chances of purchasing the lots on which they had built, at the sale.

The erection of public as well as private buildings rapidly progressed, and on the 17th day of October, 1839, President Lamar, with a portion of his cabinet, arrived in Austin. This was a day of great rejoicing among the citizens. The President was met a few miles from the city by a large procession, headed by Gen. A. Sidney Johnson (who was then Secretary of War, but had preceded the President), and Gen. Edward Burleson. Judge Waller, on behalf of the citizens, welcomed the President to the capital city in a brief but well worded address.

The arrival of the President and his party gave renewed confidence to the people; emigrants were flocking to the new city, and buildings were rapidly going up in every direction. In the latter part of October, 1839, the *Austin City Gazette* was established by Sam Whiting, and shortly afterwards another paper, called the *Sentinel*, was also established.

On the 11th of November, 1839, the first session of the Fourth Congress met at the new capital, and in a very short time commenced agitating the question of a removal of the seat of government, and finally a bill was introduced to leave the subject of removal to the people, which was very promptly voted down, notwithstanding it was zealously supported by Gen. Houston, who was then a member of Congress from San Augustine county.

Early in January, 1840, Mr. Amos Roark found the census of the city to be as follows: "Seventy-five families, population eight hundred and fifty-six, of which seven hundred and eleven were whites and one hundred and forty-five blacks—five hundred and fifty grown men, sixty-one ladies, one hundred children, seventy-seven of which are large enough to go to school; seventy-three professors of religion—seventeen Methodists, twelve Presbyterians, five Cumberland Presbyterians, eleven Episcopalians, ten Baptists and ten Roman Catholics; two organized churches—one Methodist and one Presbyterian; two Methodist preachers, one Cumberland Presbyterian and one Baptist preacher; one Sabbath school, one week day school, thirty-five mechanics, four lawyers, six doctors, six inns, nine stores, nine groceries, one billiard table, six faro banks, twenty gamblers, two silversmith shops, two printing offices and two tailor shops."

Congress having passed an act incorporating the City of Austin, an election under the charter was held January 13, 1840, and the first city officers chosen, Judge Waller being elected Mayor, under whose administration the city prospered greatly. The Supreme Court met for the first time in the city, on the day of the election for city officers, Thomas J. Rusk being Chief Justice, and James M. Robinson, John T. Mills, William J. Jones and Anthony B. Shelby, Associate Justices; William Fairfax Gray, clerk; Preston Conlee, sheriff, and after a session of thirteen days, adjourned. At the following session, in 1841, Judge Rusk having retired from the bench, Judge John Hemphill became Chief Justice, and on the 20th of January, 1841, the office of clerk being declared vacant, Gen. Thomas Green was elected and continued in the position until the breaking out of the civil war, in which he distinguished himself as an able Brigadier General in Gen. Kirby Smith's army, sacrificing his life in the gunboat engagement at Blair's Landing on Red River.

The independence of Texas had been acknowledged by the United States (that government being represented by Geo. H. Flood, at the Capital of the young Republic), England, and France. M. De Saligny, the French Minister, had also arrived in the city, and had erected one of the finest residences then in the State. About this time negotiations were pending between the Republic of Texas and France for a loan by the latter government to aid the development of Texas. Had the loan been effected, it would unquestionably have proved disastrous to the future grand career of the State. Fortunately, it was prevented by some pigs belonging to Mr. Bullock, the principal hotel-keeper in the city. The pigs were in the habit of running about the stable of the French minister, much to the annoyance of a servant who finally killed them. Mr. Bullock, in retaliation, whipped the servant, which action highly incensed the French diplomat, and as a result his conduct became so obnoxious to the Texas government that President Lamar requested his recall by France, which request was promptly complied with, thus abruptly ending M. De Saligny's career as minister plenipotentiary to the Republic of Texas, and the negotiations for the French loan, at one and the same time.

On the second Monday of December, 1841, General Sam Houston (having been elected President in the September previous), was inaugurated — that being the first and only inaugural of a President of the Republic that ever occurred in Austin. In the following spring the Mexicans invaded Texas, sacking the town of San Antonio, and causing such widespread alarm as to decide the government administration upon seeking a safer habitat — the principal archives, except those belonging to the General Land Office, being removed to Houston. These latter the citizens of Austin determined to retain, in order to secure to the city at least a portion of the general government. Several attempts were made by the administration to recover possession of these archives, but Austin pluckily held on to them, notwithstanding its people had their hands full in guarding the city from the attacks of the savages, and in rendering assistance to repel the Mexican invaders of the State. They had invested nearly a million of dollars in the city on the strength of its being the permanent Capital of the Republic, and, when the strong arm of the government was with unseemly haste withdrawn from their support, they manfully determined to protect themselves and the city, and at the same time preserve to Austin its title as the Capital by keeping within its confines one of the principal departments of the general government. They proved themselves fully equal for the trying emergencies, and but for their courage and resoluteness the great State of Texas would in all probability have been virtually deprived of its beautiful Capital City of to-day.

In the fall of 1844, Anson Jones was elected President of the Republic, a complete change of government followed his inauguration. Congress adopted measures for the annexation of Texas to the United States, and pursuant to the President's call, the convention to frame a State Constitution, assembled at Austin, July 4, 1845, the citizens having proposed, if the convention was called, to assemble at Austin, to turn over the land office archives and abide by whatever decision was rendered in regard to the matter. The convention recognized Austin as the seat of government until 1850, in which year, by a provision in the State constitution adopted, an election was to be held for the purpose of locating the capital for twenty years. An election was accordingly held on the first Monday in March, 1850, the result being in favor of Austin, although Washington, Huntsville and Tehuacana were its rivals for the honor. At the expiration of twenty years the city was declared the permanent capital of the State by an overwhelming popular vote. From the time of the annexation of Texas as a member of the Union, Austin continued to grow and improve in a very substantial manner. A complete check to its prosperity was occasioned, however, by the breaking out of the war, and in common with all other parts of the South, the city sacrificed many valuable lives, as well as considerable wealth in the struggle. After the close of that period there was no material progress made by that city, until it became fixed upon as a railway terminus. That event gave an impetus to business of every description, the effect of which is to be seen in the magnificent development of to-day. True, there has, in the meantime, been serious drawbacks to the progress of its commercial interests, due to the fact that at the period when the tendency in that direction first was greatest, the city was governed by an administration of the moss-back description, which hung like a mill-stone about the neck of the city, preventing its rise in response to the repeated calls of capital eagerly seeking to develop its many commercial advantages. With the inauguration of a new city government some five years ago, however, business at once revived, and enterprise and progress being warmly welcomed to the city, has since made wonderful strides in establishing Austin's commercial prosperity upon a broad and substantial foundation. The enthusiastic predictions of the commissioners who located Austin, concerning its future as a great emporium of trade and traffic, are being literally verified, even now, and there is no question that its commercial importance will be many times greater when the first period of fifty years of its existence expires.

Having thus briefly traced the rise of Austin from a mere hamlet composed of but three families, and situated on the extreme frontier of the crude civilization of forty years ago, to the present time, wherein it is a flourishing city of about 18,000 inhabitants, and the capital seat of by all odds the *greatest* State of the Union, let us now look at its innumerable advantages and vast resources for becoming one of the most

PROMINENT CENTERS

of trade, commerce and manufactures in Texas.

Travis County, of which Austin is the county seat, was named in honor of William Barret Travis, who fell in the cause of Texan independence, while commanding the historic little garrison that fought to the death against the overwhelming hordes of blood-thirsty Mexicans, which beseiged the doomed Alamo in 1836.

The area of the county is 1,019 square miles, and, owing to the diversity of its topography, soil and other characteristics, it is well adapted to the profitable pursuit of a great variety of industries. It combines, in fact, many of the distinctive features which separately characterize several sections of the State. From the heavily timbered hills, in some places assuming the proportion of mountains, in the Western portion, the surface slopes down to the rich alluvial bottoms of the Colorado river and the rolling prairies in the Eastern section. The cotton, grain and fruit producing lands lie side by side, and, in consequence, the landscape presents a pleasing diversity of aspect, and the products of the soil an unusual and profitable variety. The Colorado river flows through the county from West to East, in a somewhat Southerly course. It ranks first among the rivers of the State in size, but, owing to the shoals and falls in its channel, is not navigable. (In 1846 or 1847 a steamboat made the trip to Austin, and a regular navigation company was organized to clean out the river. In 1851 another steamer made her appearance at Austin, and was expected to make regular trips. The Board of Aldermen passed an ordinance establishing a regular landing, regulating wharfage and fees of wharfmaster, etc. That was the last trip of the "Colorado Ranger," or any other steamboat to Austin. It is predicted, however, that the Colorado river will yet be regularly navigated to Austin.) Along its banks are some of the most fertile and beautiful farms in the State, and also the most picturesque scenery. It pursues a zig-zag course across the county, thereby watering a large area, while the Perdernales river, in the Western corner, with a number of smaller streams flowing into the Colorado on either side, further increase the water resources of the county.

Water for drinking purposes is obtained from wells at moderate depth, but it is generally more or less impregnated with lime, in consequence of which cistern water is preferred, and very generally used.

The county, in addition to being well watered, possesses the scarcely less valuable condition of being abundantly timbered. About four-fifths of the area is more or less densely covered by a growth comprising almost every species of tree known to Texas, except the pine and sweet gum, which indeed are rarely to be found elsewhere than in the Eastern and Southeastern portions of the State. The hills and uplands abound in cedar and oak of the several kinds, while the bottoms and rolling lands are studded with the pecan, hickory, ash, walnut, elm, cypress, hackberry, bois d' arc, mesquite and cottonwood. Many of these woods possess qualities of hardness and durability which make them valuable for building, mechanical and manufacturing purposes.

The good farming lands embrace about five-eights of the area, one-fifth of which is under cultivation, the remainder being devoted to grazing, or still undisturbed forest land.

Under proper cultivation, the average yield per acre is of seed cotton, 800 to 1,000 pounds; corn, 30 bushels; wheat, 16 bushels; oats, 50 to 75 bushels; rye, 15 bushels; barley, 45 to 60 bushels; sweet potatoes, 200 bushels; Irish potatoes, 90 bushels; sorghum syrup, 3 barrels; millet, 3 tons; and prairie hay, 1 ton. Garden vegetables, melons, fruits and berries of almost every kind common to the temperate zone do well. Apples, however, have never been successfully raised, but peaches, plums and figs are particularly fine and plentiful.

Agricultural implements of the latest and most improved patterns are in general use, and the adaptation of the crop to the soil and climate is receiving increased attention. Indeed, all thing considered, the methods of agriculture in the County of Travis may be said to be as intelligent and progressive as in any portion of the South. While it is true that the native Southern farmer is still inclined to devote himself rather too exclusively to cotton culture, leaving experimental farming to others, the immigrant brings with him predilections quite as strong in favor of the staple products of the land of his birth. Thus many crops which tradition has declared unsuited to the soil and climate, have been introduced and are now successfully cultivated. Barley may be mentioned as an instance of this progress. The abundance and certainty of its yield have commended it as a valuable addition to the stock-feed products, if

not in large measure as a substitute for corn, which is not regarded as an altogether reliable crop in this section, owing to an occasional absence of plentiful
rainfall during its short critical maturing season.

Considerable attention is paid to

STOCK RAISING

in the country, either as a separate pursuit, or in connection with farming.   A
large part of the area not enclosed for farm purposes is carpeted with a luxuriant growth of mesquite grass, the most nutritious of the native grasses of
the State.   There is also the Colorado bottom grass, which springs up in the
cultivated fields in the river bottoms, and for hay is considered almost equal to
oats.   Two crops a year are grown, about three and a half tons to the acre.
Cattle, horses, mules and goats are raised on the range at small expense,
requiring but little care or attention.   Sheep also are kept for the most part of
the year on the range, but during the winter it is essential to give them more
or less feed, especially in inclement weather.   With reasonable care, they keep
in good condition, are subject to no disease, increase at the rate of sixty per
cent., and yield a fleece of four to six pounds per annum, worth in Austin, the
home market, twenty-five cents per pound.   Hogs require attention and some
feed throughout the year, otherwise they are not successfully raised on the
range.   Domestic fowls of all kinds are profitably raised, and wild game, such
as deer, turkeys, geese, ducks, quail, plover and rabbits, is abundant.   The
larger streams in the country also yield a good supply of fish, the trout and
perch being particularly fine, though not as plentiful as catfish, buffalo, fresh
water mullet and some other less dainty species of the finny tribe.

Such, in brief, are the general features, from an agricultural standpoint, of
the immediate country surrounding Austin, and that they are of an unusually
attractive order none will deny.   It must also be borne in mind that Austin
is the natural distributing market for the surplus agricultural products of a
vast scope of territory contiguous to Travis County, and which also is unsurpassed for productiveness and diversified yield by any section of the State.

WATER POWER.

Nature appears to have especially designed the site of Austin for manufacturing purposes, judging by the magnificent water power it possesses.   Just
above the city there is a fall of ten and a half feet in the Colorado river,
which, according to competent judges who have made a critical examination of
its character and the volume of water rushing over the descent, affords abundant power for propelling the machinery of a vast number of manufacturing
industries.   But a very small percentage of this power, has thus far been utilized—one flouring mill being operated by it, which though not by any means
an enterprise remarkable for its extensiveness, has nevertheless proved a
highly profitable investment to its owners, and is an ample demonstration of

what other manufacturers can do.   And unquestionably this grand water power will be utilized to its utmost limit by manufacturing capital in a very short period of time, now that its advantages are known to have been thoroughly tested by practical men, and the rapid development of the city since its acquirement of the many essential artificial facilities, makes it a field so especially inviting to that class of industries which relies chiefly upon cheap motive power for success.

COAL.

The abundant timber growth in the vicinity of Austin insures the city an ample fuel supply for ordinary purposes for many years to come, and at cheap rates.   But for generating steam and the various manufacturing purposes, it is absolutely necessary for an abundant supply of coal to be available to a city, and a supply too, that is of a superior quality and low-priced.   It has been the lack of this most essential commodity and its immense cost, that has so retarded the growth of manufacturing industries in Texas.   This serious obstruction, however, is now rapidly being removed by the development of the coal measures of the State, which scientific explorations have demonstrated to be so vast in quantity, excellent in quality, and so available to every section of the State, that there is no longer a question of doubt as to the ability of Texas to furnish all the coal necessary for its own wants—manufacturing or otherwise—but to produce a large surplus each year for export.

Austin is peculiarly fortunate in having an inexhaustible supply located just without its gateways, in what is known as the

ROCKDALE COAL MINES.

The extensive coal field, owned and operated by the Austin and Central Texas Coal Company, is situated on the International and Great Northern Railway, in Milan County, only 61 miles from the city.   The first vein occurs 40 feet below the surface, and is six feet thick.   Another vein, twelve inches in thickness, is found 31 feet below the first vein, the seams being interstratified with one foot of excellent fire-clay, 13 feet of sand, one foot of augite and 15 feet of clay.   At a further depth of 6 feet of clay occurs a third seam of coal, 7 feet 6 inches thick, overlying a very superior bed of fire-clay, beneath which explorations have not gone.   These mines have been defined as covering an area of 250 acres in extent, without making a single break, and the interlying formations so far as reached, indicates a large number of seams before striking the bottom rocks, commonly known as mill-stone grit; thus justifying the opinion that the Rockdale coal beds are for all practical purposes simply exhaustless.   The coal is bituminous, of the cannel variety, ignites easily, burns with a very bright flame and has a specific gravity of 1.33.   An analysis made by Professor Dinwiddle, shows the following to be its component properties: Ash, 6,565; sulpher, 2,880; hydro-carbon, nitrogen, and oxygen gasses, 90,555.

The Professor, in reporting this showing, says: "This result is reliable and makes the coal very valuable, and destined to soon come into active demand in Texas. I am sure it will make a cheap and good gas."

The closing assertion of the Professor, as to its gas producing qualities, is fully sustained by the following comparative test, reported by Mr. C. M. Holmes, Superintendent of the Austin Gas Works: "After a careful test of your coal as to the quantities of gases it contains, I find it to compare with other coals as follows, in feet of gas obtained from a pound of coal: Rockdale, .650; McAllister, (Indian Territory) 4.50; Pittsburg, 4.10. The residual products in the Rockdale coal are comparatively worthless."

Upon this basis the following comparison in the relative values for the manufacture of gas of the Rockdale and McAllister coals speaks for itself:

ROCKDALE.

2,000 lbs. coal yield 13,000 feet of gas, at $4.00	$52.00
Coke	
Tar	
Deduct cost of coal	5.00
Net value	$47.00

McALLISTER.

2,000 lbs. coal yield 9,000 feet of gas, at $4.00	$36.00
Coke, ⅔ ton, at $8.50	5.66
Tar, 36 gallons at 12½c	4.50
Total	$46.16

Deduct $7.50, cost of coal, and there remains a balance of $8.34 in favor of the home product at Rockdale, which fact alone is sufficient to commend it to Superintendents of Texas gas works and other manufacturers as well.

The opening up of these magnificent deposits of light and heat, that have been slumbering in the bosom of the earth for untold centuries cannot fail of adding materially to the future resources of the State, while the influence therefrom bearing directly upon the prosperity of this city is so obvious as to make further comment superfluous.

With the coal interests of Texas fully developed, we will see manufacturing interests of every kind and character springing up throughout the State. Particularly will this be the case in the matter of

IRON,

the ore of which exists in inexhaustible quantities and at so many different points as to make not alone the numerous particular sections in which it abounds, but the entire State, feel a keen interest in the development of this latent resource which, like a sleeping giant, now is to arouse up in the not distant future and wield its mighty power in promoting the prosperity of Texas. There is iron ore, pronounced by such competent and learned scientists as Dr. Shumard, formerly State Geologist, the late Professor Boll, of Dallas, and several other well known authorities, as being identical with the renowned gray ore of England and Wales, in this State alone, sufficient to supply the United States for generations, for every purpose for which iron and steel may be needed. With the erection of an adequate number of furnaces, rolling mills and foundries in Texas (as there will be in a very little while), the railroads already built in our State, and those yet to be built, will be able to have supplied them all the iron and steel rails they may need, all the bolts, fish plates, wheels, axles and ironing for their cars, made on the spot from the raw material produced in Texas, thus saving the immense costs of transportation they now have to pay ; the farmer will have manufactured at his very doors, as it were, every description of farming machinery and implements he may require, and, in short, every known article fashioned out of iron or steel and which (except to a very limited extent) we are now compelled to import, will be manufactured in the State of Texas out of the ore produced by Texas. Reference to any comprehensive work on the mineral resources of the State, will show that every county in which coal has been found also abounds in iron, for it seems to be an invariable fact that wherever, in the aiembic of nature, one of the minerals has been formed, the other is close by. Vulcan and his forge would be useless without proper fuel, which alone is coal, and a beneficent nature rarely, if ever, gives iron ore without coal. Extensive deposits of iron ore are known to exist in the vicinity of Austin, and now that the development of the coal formations in this section have actively commenced, the development of the iron will naturally follow, and there is good reasons to believe it will not long be delayed. Enterprising capital is continually on the alert in this ever restless pushing country of ours, and the opportunity for profitable investment does not long remain without a claimant. And as an evidence of the favorable opportunities which await iron manufacturing capital in Austin, it is only necessary to direct the readers' attention to the immense iron ore deposits of Llano county. About 12 miles from the town of Llano, there is a massive iron hill 30 feet high above its visible base, 800 feet long and 500 feet wide, and 300 feet above the surface of the Llano river at low water mark. It is a solid compact mass of iron ore which has been tested and found to yield 70 per cent. of pure iron (some specimens have assayed as high as 95 per cent.), whereas 50 per cent. is considered an excellent yield in the Pennsylvania mines ; and, moreover, this ore from the iron mountain of Llano county is identical with the best quality of Swedish iron. Immense blocks of iron ore are scattered profusely around the base of the hill; and not only are timber and good water plentiful about it, but limestone rocks of the paleozoic and cretaceous descriptions exist in abundance.

Eight miles distant to the northwest is a large bed of magnetic iron ore, situated between two ridges of granite. The untold thousands of tons of iron in this region are only about 80 miles from the City of Austin, and they will soon be placed at our very doors, as it were, by the extension (now in progress) of the Austin & Northwestern railway, from its present terminus at Burnet, 60 miles distant from Austin. Vast beds of iron ore also exist in San Saba County, 90 miles northwest of Austin, and on the projected line of the same railway just mentioned.

Possessed of such rare advantages, can anyone doubt that Austin will eventually become a great iron manufacturing point?

It is also interesting to note that the city has an abundance of

COPPER

at its control. Llano County, where iron ore is plentiful, is equally as prolific in copper ore. Prof. Steeruwitz says: "I found near the surface copper ores—peacock ore, blue and green carbonate—assaying 56 per cent. of copper, besides 87 ounces of silver to the ton, and strong traces of gold, and outcrops of gray copper ore, with 627 ounces of silver to the ton; and I traced this copper belt from the northern part of Llano County through Burnet, Mason and Menard Counties." "Owens' mine," at the head of Pecan Creek, in Llano County, is now worked with improved machinery, and the ore being taken out assays $300 worth of pure copper to the ton.

SILVER BEARING LEAD ORES,

mostly galena, also crop out in Llano County and can be easily traced to San Saba and Burnet Counties, in which latter county, near Bluffton, old Spanish shafts and tunnels still exist.

BUILDING STONE,

of every description exists in abundance throughout the State—the marbles, limestones, and gray and red granites being unexcelled in qualities by any of the famed productions of the world, as may be readily demonstrated by the specimens used in the construction of the magnificent capitol building now in course of erection at Austin, the material for which is obtained from quarries almost within sight of the capital city. Layers of

MARBLE,

of different colors, and rare and beautiful varieties are found in extensive formations along the Colorado River. Of the specimens contributed by this section to the collection gathered by the agent of the United States Census Bureau, the agent in charge says: "We consider them very beautiful, and have dressed them with much care. They are mineralogically interesting, and different from any other marble in our collection." At what is known as Marble Falls, in Burnet County, the Colorado River makes an abrupt descent of about 100 feet over a solid bed of marble. The deposit along this stream varies in tint from the purest white to jet black, and is highly valuable for building purposes, ornamental or statuary work. The mountains in Llano County, in many places, are composed of

SOLID GRANITE.

Burnet County is also prolific in gray and red granites, the latter believed to be identical with the celebrated Scotch granite. Blanco County, too, abounds in granite and marble. These vast deposits of marble, granite and limestones, lying the counties of Blanco, Burnet, Llano and San Saba, are within a radius of from 50 to 100 miles of Austin, and the city is, or shortly will be, in direct communication with them through the medium of the Austin & Northwestern Railway. That the working of marble and granite will become a large and profitable industry in the city in the near future, is, in fact, assured by the progress already made in that direction by the enterprising spirits engaged in laying its foundations.

But further details concerning Austin's advantages by reason of its contiguity to the raw material furnished by Nature's mineral storehouses, is unnecessary, for it is now a well known fact that the mineral resources of Texas cannot be surpassed by any State in the Union, in variety, quantity and quality, and it is equally apparent, from its geographical location, that no city in the Lone Star State is more eligibly situated with reference to easy accessibility to these endless mines of wealth than the capital city—Austin.

TRANSPORTATION FACILITIES.

The actual progress of a city, no matter how varied and extensive its natural advantages may be, must always be measured by the character and scope of its transportation facilities. And more particularly is this true concerning a city without widely extending navigable water-ways at its command. The Colorado River, upon which the city of Austin is located, ranks first among the rivers of the State in size, but, unfortunately, owing to the shoals and falls in its channel that stream is not navigable, and it is useless to attempt to conceal the fact that to make it so, would involve such an enormous expenditure of money, that in all probability its improvement to that extent will never be undertaken. And, furthermore, however desirable such an end would be to this city, it could scarcely be considered the part of wisdom to do so, not alone for reasons quite obvious from a manufacturing standpoint, but in view of the far more efficient method for transportation at our command in the form of

RAILROADS,

and the wonderful progress science is continually making in the improvement of their standard. That they are infinitely superior to all other carrier systems is now a fact too well established to be controverted, and each year increases the public confidence in their developing influence upon the world at large, and in no section of it so particularly as in America. They bring immigration to a new country, cause new towns and villages to spring up; make towns and cities already in existence to grow and increase in material prosperity, and give a stimulus to every resource of the land through which they pass. They are, in the highest sense, the advance guards of civilization, and they foster and encourage not only civilization, progress and development themselves, but create a corresponding tendency in their every adjunct.

The claims that railroads make a State, in so far as concerns Texas, is a matter by no means difficult to substantiate. It is verified at once by the marvelous growth of railroading itself in the State during the past fifteen years. At the close of the war in 1865, there was less than 300 miles of railroad, and of that small mileage, but little outside of the seventy miles operated by the Houston and Texas Central, between Houston and Navasota, and the fifty miles belonging to the Galveston, Houston and Henderson line, was of any importance. The State, in common with all the Southern States at that period, being financially prostrated, the people being poor and having to commence at the bottom once more to find a comfortable living, and immigration being only a thing in name, there was little or no encouragement for railroad enterprises, and less capital for investment in them. Still, the roads then in the State were not disheartened, and though their progress was naturally quite slow, at the close of the first five years after the war we had about 500 miles of railway lines, the whole of which was in very excellent running condition. In 1870 the railroad boom struck the State fairly and squarely, and, as a result, in the extent of railroad mileage, Texas to-day ranks as Sixth among the States, with over 6,000 miles, increased from 865 miles in 1871. What its rank will be ten years hence may be surmised from the following comparison of railroad growth in the six States having the greatest mileage at this date, during the past fourteen years:

STATES.	MILES OF RAILROAD.	
	1871.	1884.
Illinois	5,901	9,068
New York	4,742	7,369
Pennsylvania	3,740	7,488
Ohio	4,476	7,322
Iowa	3,160	7,405
Texas	855	6,147

Austin was one of the first important points in the State to feel the beneficial effects of the railroad boom, and, literally speaking, whatever progress it
has made since then, and its present bright prospects, are due solely to its railway connections, which places it in direct communication with every section
of the State, and makes it readily accessible by through lines from any point
in the Union.

The pioneer road to enter the Capital City, was the

HOUSTON AND TEXAS CENTRAL,

in 1871, which in December of that year completed its branch, then called the
"Austin Air Line Branch," extending from Hempstead, 115 miles east of Austin, on the main stem of the H. & T. C., but now known as the

WESTERN DIVISION

of that road. By this line of railway, Austin is placed within 166 miles of
Houston, and 216 miles of the gulf port of Galveston. The Houston & Texas
Central is the oldest railway system in the State, having been chartered March
11, 1848, and as its name indicates, the road traverses the very heart of Texas,
the trunk line extending north from Houston on the gulf coast, to Denison on
the Red River slopes, a distance of 338 miles, while through its extensive
branches, and the numerous other lines with which it makes close connection,
it penetrates every portion of the State, making it upon the whole, one of the
important trunk railways in the entire country. The total mileage operated
by the system is as follows:

Main Line (Houston to Denison) ....338 miles.
Western Division (Hempstead to Austin) 115   "
Northwestern Division (Bremond to Albany) 221   "
Northeastern Division (Garrett to Roberts) 52   "
Waxahachie Division (Garrett to Waxahachie) 12   "

Total mileage...................................738 miles.

The Missouri Pacific connections and the northwestern division feeds it
with cattle shipped to the gulf, but the western division has the greatest cotton
tonnage of all, as it passes through the wealthy and populous farming region,
embracing the Colorado and Brazos River Valleys.

INTERNATIONAL & GREAT NORTHERN RAILWAY.

The International & Great Northern Railway entered Austin January 1,
1877, and as an energetic and enterprising competitor for its passenger and
freight traffic, has proved a valuable adjunct in the development of the city.

This road—which constitutes one of the most important factors in the
great Missouri—Pacific trunk system—was created by the consolidation, Sept.
22, 1873, of the International, chartered August 17, 1870, and opened to Long-

view, distant from Houston 232 miles, and 81 miles from Palestine, in December 1872, and the Houston & Great Northern, chartered October 22, 1866, and opened to Palestine, 151 miles distant from Houston, in 1872. Longview is the terminus of the main line, which, since the Galveston, Houston & Henderson Railway came under control of the Missouri-Pacific system, has been termed the Gulf Division.

The old line chartered as the Houston, Tap & Brazoria Railway, Sept. 1, 1856, and completed in 1860, was purchased by the Houston & Great Northern Company in 1871, and of course now forms a part of the consolidation of the International & Great Northern, and consequently is also embraced in the Missouri-Pacific system. This road pierces the great sugar district of Texas, extending from Houston to Columbia, a distance of 50 miles, and is an important feeder to the commerce of the entire State.

The International & Great Northern now operates 825 miles of road (all of which lies within the State), as follows:

Main Line—Long view to Galveston....................282 miles.
Henderson Branch—Overton to Henderson 16   "
Mineola   "   —Troupe to Mineola 44   "
San Antonio Division—Palestine to Laredo 415   "
Georgetown Branch—Round Rock to Georgetown 10   "
Huntsville   "   —Phelps to Huntsville............... 8   "
Columbia   "   —Houston to Columbia 50   "

            Total ....825 miles.

The San Antonio division passes directly through Austin on its way to Laredo, on the Rio Grande, 234 miles distant, where it connects with the Mexican system of railways. The distance of San Antonio to the Capital City is 80 miles, and while this division of the road enables us to draw, without limit, upon the vast wealth of that region prolific in agricultural and pastoral products, it also brings to our doors the multifarious products of the eastern sections of the State, and affords one of the most exhaustive outlets for our own surplus products. In fact, through this division of the International & Great Northern Railway, Austin has command of the entire 6,045 miles of railway now being operated by the system known as the

MISSOURI PACIFIC RAILWAY COMPANY,

and which embraces the Missouri Pacific Railway proper; St. Louis, Iron Mountain & Southern Railway; Missouri, Kansas & Texas Railway; International & Great Northern Railroad; Galveston, Houston & Henderson Railroad; Texas & Pacific Railway; Central Branch Union Pacific Railway, and Sedalia, Warsaw & Southern Railroad. The ramifications of this vast system of railway lines in the States of Texas, Louisiana, Arkansas, Missouri, Nebraska,

Kansas and the Indian Territory, are of the most important as well as extensive character, and the advantages derived from it by the Capital City are incomparably great.

AUSTIN & NORTHWESTERN RAILWAY.

The Austin & Northwestern Railway, which is now being rapidly pushed in the direction its name indicates, is destined to become one of the most important of Austin's main arteries of commerce, as it cannot fail to be the means of largely augmenting the general trade of the city, by opening up the wide extent of fertile and growing country to the North and West. Its initial point is Austin, and it may well be called, strictly speaking, a Colorado River railway, as it clings to the rich shores of that grand stream throughout its entire route as projected thus far. The line as surveyed, traverses the counties of Travis, Williamson, Burnet, Lampasas, Brown and Coleman, in the order named, crossing the Brushy and Gabriel Rivers on its route, and passes through not only some of the finest agricultural land in the State, but its way lies through a region of untold mineral wealth.

Coleman County, in which the extreme northwestern point to which the line of survey has reached is located, lies in the belt of country west of a line running from the mouth of Little Wichita, on the Red River, to the mouth of Pecan Bayou, on the Colorado River, which, according to competent geologists, discloses unmistakable indications of true coal formation, and also of the best quality of iron ore. Brown County lies in the same geological belt, and in addition to coal and iron, contains copper, silver and lead, and also petroleum in large quantities—two wells in Brownwood (the county seat) at a depth of from 90 to 120 feet, yield 80 per cent. of pure oil.

Lampasas County is noted for its numerous white sulphur and chalybeate springs, the waters of which possess valuable medicinal properties. The principal of these, the Hanna and Hancock Springs, each have a flow of 1,000 gallons per minute. The Lampasas springs are not only patronized to a very great extent by invalids, but their combined natural and artificial attractions are of such a character as to make them extremely popular as a resort at all seasons for pleasure-seekers and tourists generally. The general elevation is about 1,200 feet above the sea level, and from the tops of the hills near at hand a beautiful and varied panorama of valleys, streams and fields is presented, and much of the mountain scenery is picturesque and grand. They are situated near the town of Lampasas, the county seat, and are 65 miles northwest of the Capital City.

Burnett County possesses iron ore, and, to a less extent, lead, gold and silver; but its most prominent features, and by far its most valuable, from a utilitarian point of view, are its immense deposits of limestone of superior quality; its gray and red granites, the latter identical with the Scotch granite;

and its vast beds of marble, varying in tint from pure white to jet black, many of the shades being particularly rare and beautiful. These granites and marbles are pronounced by government experts at Washington City, after having subjected specimens to scientific tests, to be equal to the best American or imported stone of the kinds. They are largely used in the Capital building now under construction in our city. Burnet, the county seat, sixty miles distant from Austin, is the present terminus of the Austin and Northwestern.

In Williamson County (the county next adjoining Travis County on the line of the Austin and Northwestern), iron ore, silver and petroleum are known to exist, and there are surface indications of coal, but the extent of the deposits have not yet been determined. The county is rapidly becoming noted for its valuable wool clip, sheep-raising now being conducted upon a very large scale, particular attention being paid to the highest-improved breeds. The largest single clip of wool from one sheep, exhibited at the International Cotton Exposition at Atlanta, Ga., in 1881, was the fleece of a Williamson County sheep. It weighed forty-four pounds, and the same animal yielded for five years an average of thirty-five pounds and one ounce of wool per annum. An abundance of the raw material right in the adjoining county, at once suggests Austin as a highly advantageous site for wool manufacturing, to say nothing of its contributions to the commerce of our city now that the Austin and Northwestern gives the wool-growers of that community a direct and speedy transit for their product to Austin's market.

The counties bordering upon those through which the main line of the Austin and Northwestern Railway is surveyed, are equally noted for their abundant and varied products, and as rapidly as the main stem is extended, they will undoubtedly be made more directly tributary to both the road and Austin, by the construction of branch lines. In fact, the benefits which Austin will derive from this line of railway will be of the most substantial character, and while we make all proper allowance for any exaggeration of the extent of the future benefits that the present highly flattering prospects may occasion, it is palpably plain that the intrinsic value of the Austin and Northwestern Railway to the Capital of the State will prove far greater than the conservative minded who put their entire faith in the road now anticipate.

There are several other lines of railway in contemplation, but inasmuch as they have not yet arrived at that stage of maturity that warrants their being called established facts, though ultimately they will become such, it is unnecessary to consume space in outlining their proposed routes. With the three well equipped railroads already in active operation—two of which are great trunk lines ramifying every section of the State and affording the most thorough systems of direct communication with all parts of the Union—and the city being the center of an extensive territory, the trade of which is otherwise unprovided for, there is no longer a question for doubt that Austin has promising and perhaps more permanent guarantees of commercial, and also manufacturing greatness, than many more pretentious and demonstrative cities in Texas.

COMMERCIAL INTERESTS.

Amid the many other and more engaging attractions peculiar to the Capital of the State, its business interests have never been accorded the prominent attention of the public to which, from their character and extent, they seem justly entitled. However, this apparent indifference has in no wise deterred the march of progress, and through the quiet, but none the less vigorous, enterprise of our merchants the city's commercial prosperity is being steadily and surely advanced, each year showing a marked improvement upon the record of the preceding one, and determining more positively the future greatness of Austin as a business center. A fair illustration of the energetic spirit controlling in the business circles, is to be seen in the amount of freight handled at this point by the railways entering the city. During the season of 1883-84 the amount handled was placed at 292,000,000 pounds, or 146,000 tons, an increase of about 10,000 tons on the freight operations of the previous fiscal year, while this season it is estimated the aggregate will reach fully 160,000 tons, if the total tonnage does not exceed that figure.

Another evidence of our commercial progress, is found in the marked growth of the city as a

COTTON

market. For the season ending in 1882, the shipments of cotton from Austin were placed at 24,000 bales. The figures put down for the past season fixes the shipments at 46,000 bales, an increase of over 90 per cent. in two years.

To the close observer of the active movements of our cotton men of late, sufficient evidence is discovered to show that the work of development in the proper direction has actually begun and that the outlook of this principal factor in the city's ultimate distinguished position among the royally appointed commercial centers of the Western hemisphere, was never so promising as at present. Now that we have a cotton compress—that mighty and indispensible adjunct for perfecting the facilities for handling the fleecy staple advantageously, it is safe to predict that the Capital City is entering an era of prosperity to which it has hitherto been a stranger, and which will improve under the judicious management of spirited and progressive enterprise to a degree unparalled in the experience of Southern cities.

The

COTTON COMPRESS,

of which we speak, and to which must be largely attributed the rapid increase of cotton receipts and shipments at this point, has a capacity of 600 bales per

day. The company operating it was incorporated in 1883, with a capital stock
of $50,000. The inauguration of this most valuable commercial enterprise,
establishes the fact that, that element of dash long underlying the business
movements of the city, has reached the surface, and upon the crested wave of
progress it is rolling onward to the haven of success. The controlling power
has been assumed by the younger, and the more vigorous business men, and
"old fogyism," realizing that its sway has virtually ended, will speedily disap-
pear forver, its dismal croakings and cadaverous form only being recalled to
memory to more forcibly illustrate to future generations the grand results of
ambitious life ruled by advanced progress. Austin's future is in safe hands—
hands strong and willing, and impelled to constant doing by the warm and
enthusiastic blood of hearts full of faith and courage. *Its success is assured.*

WOOL.

The shipments of wool, which two years ago were estimated at 975,000
pounds, now reach about one and a quarter million pounds. The contiguity
of Austin to the wool growing sections of the State and its excellent facilities
for handling this invaluable product, guarantees our wool market a future prosperity that will be scarcely excelled by that of our cotton interests.

HIDES

also constitute an important factor in the commerce of Austin, on account of
its favorable advantages as a distributing point. Probably not less than 400,-
000 pounds per annum are now handled in this market and the steady growth
of operations augurs a future in which the extent will scarcely have a limit.

The annual shipments of cattle are about 20,000 head ; sheep, 2,000 head ;
horses, 1,200 head. With such other commodities as cotton seed, hay, pecans,
and general agricultural products, the total value of shipments closely approx-
imate $2,000,000.

This aggregate, however, does not include the transactions in

LUMBER,

which, inclusive of shipments and the local trade, amounts to fully $2,000,000
per annum. It is thus seen that the commerce of Austin in the surplus products of the territory tributary to its markets, will foot up the very handsome
sum of nearly four million dollars per annum, a creditable showing, indeed,
for an interior market, and which is also surrounded by the innumerable
absorbing influences naturally belonging to the great political center of the
State.

But there are even more striking evidences of its business development to
be seen in what are strictly termed the

MERCANTILE INTERESTS

of the city, and into which enter, chiefly, those commodities we import, to be distributed in job lots to the terrritory making Austin its base of supply, and to the local consumers through the retail channels of trade.

Among the more important of these interests are

GROCERIES.

The last statistics of Austin's commerce published about two years ago, showed the total valuation of the grocery trade to be $2,500,000. If it has only increased 20 per cent. since then, it now amounts to $3,000,000 per annum, though we are strongly inclined to believe that this estimate of increase would prove rather under the actual figures, could there be a correct statement of the trades operations compiled, which unfortunately is not possible, owing to the lack of complete data.

This difficulty of securing full and reliable information is not peculiar to the grocery trade alone, however. It prevails in every branch of business—mercantile and manufacturing—because of there being as yet no board of trade, or other organization established, to make a special feature of compiling the most complete and authentic statistics of the entire business interests of the city. As long as this lack of a body corporated together for the purpose of advancing the several trade and industrial interests of the city by the most comprehensive methods familiar to this intelligent age continues, there will exist the difficulty of obtaining complete data showing the annual value of any particular one branch of trade, either commerce or manufactures, or the total value of our business interests combined. It is to be hoped, however, that the progressive spirit which now pervades all circles of trade will speedily develop the improvement herein suggested, thereby greatly facilitating business operations of every description, mutually benefitting all alike, and rendering far more gratifying the task of those who undertake to exhibit to the public at home and abroad, the substantial advancement of the Capital City of Texas as an important business center of the country.

DRY GOODS.

Like groceries, dry goods are staple commodities of life and occupy a ruling position in trade. The business men who have control of this interest in Austin have exhibited the highest order of executive ability and the most vigorous energy in building up the dry goods trade, thereby stamping themselves as well worthy of the grand success they have attained. By their skillful judgment in selecting stocks suitable for their trade, enterprising methods of doing business, and untiring efforts to accommodate buyers in the minutest particulars, the Capital City is now one of the best dry goods markets in the State. That the trade naturally tributary to this point finds the market here fully as advantageous as either Houston or Galveston in point of prices and qualities and varieties of stocks to select from, and superior when freight tare

are considered, need no other confirmation than the rapidly increasing operations of our dry goods houses, which amounts now to over one million dollars
per annum.

BOOTS AND SHOES.

The boot and shoe trade is not more ably represented in any city of the
State than in Austin, our merchants engaged in the business being fully alive
to the wants of the people in the line of footwear, prompt in introducing the
most improved grades of goods, and keenly enterprising in their efforts to
build up the trade of this market. That they are meeting with eminent success is to be seen in the substantial growth of the business which has reached
such an extent as to justify the establishment of a manufactory that is turning out work fully equal to the best boots and shoes made in the North, both
in quality and prices.

The trade in

HATS AND CAPS,

and gent's furnishing goods, forms a growing interest in the general make-up
of the city's business. These kindred lines are carried in combination, the
stocks being very complete in variety and quality, and dealers can purchase
as advantageously here as in the markets of Houston or Galveston. A very
thriving trade has been built up by the merchants handling these goods, who
are greatly encouraged in their enterprising efforts by the success attending
their commendable labors.

DRUGS.

The drug trade of Austin exhibits a solidity of growth—the result of the
sterling enterprise engaged in it—that makes it take rank with that of any
other city in Texas. The annual sales reach between $350,000 and $400,000.
The stocks carried embrace complete lines of pure and fresh drugs and
chemicals, paints, oils, glass and the usual variety of kindred goods belonging
to this department of trade, thus guaranteeing to buyers every advantage to
be found in the markets of the great cities farther removed from home.

MISCELLANEOUS.

Without going into further specific details of the trade of Austin in our
limited space, to the exclusion of other features equally as important to the
general prosperity of the city, we conclude this portion of our work by sum-
ming up under the head of "miscellaneous," the various other branches of
trade conducted by our enterprising merchants, embracing books and stationery, confections, china, crockery and glassware, cigars and tobacco, clothing,
furniture, jewelry, millinery goods, notions, and the almost innumerable host
of lines belonging to the mercantile departments. The statement that anyone
of these branches is ably conducted, vigorously growing and annually contrib-

uting in a marked degree to the importance of the city as a commercial center, is but a reflex of what is equally true concerning all the other branches. Suffice to say, then, that in each and every department of trade there is found sterling industry, a progressive spirit, untiring energy and continual activity, and a satisfying prosperity that can only be enjoyed through commendable enterprise backed by strict business integrity. And it can be further said with truth and pride, that as a wholesale point for the establishment of any branch of commerce, no city in the State can boast advantages superior to those controlled by the Capital City, and under which favorable influences its honor, wealth and enduring greatness are gradually and assuredly being developed to the fullest maturity.

MANUFACTURING INTERESTS.

The advantages for manufacturing interests in Austin, as we have already shown, are eminently grand and prominent, and the only matter for astonishment is in their not having been more fully utilized long ago. The one chief reason, of course, is to be found in the fact that the South, prior to the war, was distinctly an agricultural seat, and only in very recent years has turned thoughts and energies to the development of the hitherto dormant resources that are now, through intelligent manipulation, working such a complete revolution in the entire political economy of the good old "Southland."

But that reason alone will not satisfy the thoughtful observer of Austin's possibilities as a manufacturing center. In looking at the innumerable evidences of thrift, genius, enterprise and pronounced ability, fully up to the standard of the times, the astonishment becomes even greater, that, in all the years *since* the war, this progression has been developing, yet still there is such vast resources in Austin's very door-yard, awaiting the magic touch of the manufacturing hand to leap into active life and quicken the pulse beats of every industry and avenue of trade in the city.

True, the work of developing manufactures here has reached an extent calculated to arouse pride and enthusiasm when contemplating the promising future, but the city has not done its entire duty in this respect, partly—and upon this score there is justification—through lack of capital in the past. In the main, however, it is because upon the one hand there has been too much importance attached to its position as the political center of the State, and upon the other hand a too absorbing interest manifested in the development of the city's commercial interests. This latter feature constituted, however, a laudable enterprise, and one, too, that amounted to a duty of the gravest character. But by investing the entire energies in the one channel, there has been an inexcusable neglect of the other opportunities, equally as inviting, and which it was equally incumbent upon the city to take advantage of and secure the vast benefits nature has lavishly placed at its command. In other words, for example, there has been too much time devoted to *commerce* in cotton, to the entire neglect of the *manufacture* of cotton. For the time being there was no apparent evil effect from this one-sided policy, but now that there is an awakening interest manifested abroad to our manufacturing advantages, the folly of the past is making itself felt, and as the city is fast obtaining to an exalted place through its promising commercial future, this deficit in manufactures disturbs that perfect equipoise essential to the success of business and the preservation of dignity in a truly great center of trade.

However, it is gratifying to note that the era of manufacturing in Austin has been ushered in, even though so much valuable time has been lost, and the vigorous enterprise which attends it augurs well for a future of grand success. But the best evidence of the present extent and the future possibilities of manufacturing at this point, can be gathered from a brief glance at the principal industries which—as noble heroes in the advance guard—have laid first claim upon our manufacturing advantages, and are now enjoying the highest order of prosperity. In doing so, however, we must bear in mind that the space of this work is limited in order that the object in view may not be hampered in securing the greatest possible success, and thereby benefiting the entire community.

COTTON SEED OIL.

Though as yet Austin cannot boast of having in its midst an industrial enterprise engaged in the manufacture of cotton goods, it can point with considerable pride to its cotton seed oil mills, which though not as extensive as some others in the State, have no superior as regards the *quality* of products, the grades of oil comparing favorably with the output of any similar manufactory in the United States. No other industry affords more pointed evidence of the power of the New South as a manufacturing center than that industry —now established in every Southern State—engaged in producing from cotton seed mammoth quantities of oil, which in the crude and refined states, are quoted as standard articles of commerce in the markets of the world, and which, by reason of its multitudinous useful properties, is of such special value as to be well nigh indispensible to the human race. In entering this worthy field of manufactures, Austin exhibits most excellent judgment, and as it possesses the necessary skill and capital, and has an abundance of the raw material at immediate command, there is no question of its future importance as a producer of cotton seed oil.

MARBLE WORKS.

The vast quarries of marble in the vicinity of Austin, the exceptional fineness as well as durability, and the rare beauty of their products, are sufficient guarantees that the Capital City is destined to take the leading rank in this line of industries. No other city in the Union has such magnificent advantages, as in the preceding pages devoted to the resources of Austin, has been clearly pointed out; and though the work of development is only as yet in the stage of infancy, progressive enterprise is in the field, laboring dilligently and most vigorously, and the outcome will be tersely expressed by the one word "Excelsior." The superiority of the work turned out by our manufacturers in marble, is amply demonstrated by the fact that the trade reaches throughout the State of Texas and heavy orders from Mexico are also placed here.

GRANITE

cutting is also destined to become one of the prominent industries of the city, the inexhaustible supply of the raw material in the neighborhood and its unexcelled qualities for building purposes, together with the perfect facilities for transportation, places us far in advance of all competitors. Now that Texas is making such remarkable progress in the erection of substantial buildings, the granite cutting interests of Austin are bound to develop in a corresponding measure. That the skill and ability necessary to supply the most exacting demands are here, needs no confirmation at our hands. The magnificent buildings, in which the highest order of architectural and mechanical skill are displayed, now adorning the beautiful Capital City, are the best evidences of that important fact.

The superabundance of the limestone formations in the vicinity of Austin makes the manufacture of

LIME,

one of our most profitable industries. Not only is the demand for home consumption fully supplied by the home product, but large quantities for shipment are also manufactured.

BRICK MANUFACTURING.

The substantial progress made by our brick manufacturers, testifies alike to their skill and the excellent qualities of the raw material found in this neighborhood. The increasing demand for the product of our manufacture, together with the spirited enterprise displayed by those engaged in the business, leaves no room to doubt the future prosperity of the industry at this point.

IRON MANUFACTURES.

That the iron manufacturing interests have not failed to recognize the valuable character of Austin's advantages for that class of industry, and are profiting by the special inducements offered, is a fact quite apparent from the extensive

FOUNDRIES AND MACHINE SHOPS,

and various other iron working establishments located in the city. Our foundries produce a wide range of castings, which, together with the excellency of the machinery built by our manufacturers, makes us quite independent in the several lines of their products; and as the work turned out compares favorably with that of Northern establishments in variety and finish, a valuable home trade has sprung up which is yearly augmenting as our facilities for manufacture are constantly being increased, by the introduction of new capital and the expanding of those establishments which have already obtained a successful standing. The various branches of the iron manufacturing industries, including those which utilize more extensively as the principal raw material, copper, zinc, tin, and the metal alloys, are ably represented in Austin, but the field is large, and like industries to an almost unlimited number can enter it and enjoy prosperity to an unusual degree through well displayed skill and enterprise. Austin wants them and cordially invites them to come; and the more capable they are financially, the better for the city and the State, generally, for large manufacturing establishments bring into the State large numbers of consumers, which in turn create a demand for an increased number of producers and both draw merchants to keep revolving the wheels of commerce, and make doubly assured the greatest possible prosperity for all alike.

FLOURING MILLS.

The manufacture of flour in the City of Austin, though as yet an interest of no great magnitude compared with the extent it has reached in some of our Texas cities, is nevertheless a growing industry which has taken a firm root and in the course of a very few years cannot fail to develop into one of the most important that Austin will boast of with just feelings of pride. There are two milling plants now established, one using steam and the other water power—the latter utilizing the munificent supply furnished by the Colorado River. Both mills are enjoying a lucrative trade, and have the satisfaction of seeing their business annually reaching greater proportions through the superior merits of the popular brands of breadstuff they are turning out.

The encouragement which these pioneers of the flouring industry in Austin are receiving, is justly deserved by the enterprise they have exhibited, and it furthermore establishes as an incontrovertible fact, that as a milling point, capital can desire no more favorable location. Water power is here in abundance which can be utilized 365 days in the year, and coal is now even more plentiful for creating steam power if preferred. The prolific agricultural country surrounding Austin and its extensive railway system, placing within its reach every wheat-growing section of the State, insures a continuous supply of the raw material; and finally, there is the market for the product—no matter how vast it might become Texas alone can consume it entire. The fact is, there is no manufacturing interest now in the State of more importance—to the extent of its growth—than the manufacture of wheat into flour and bran. At least three-fourths of the flour which we consume comes from Kansas, Missouri, California, and other States north, and yet the annual product of wheat in the State will average twenty million bushels, worth at home about 80 cents per bushel, or a total of $16,000,000. Two-thirds of this yield is shipped North, by which disposition the bran and coarser grades of flour are nearly a complete loss, the cost of transportation being almost equal to the market value—amounting to a total deprivation of our people of those commodities. The cost of shipping our wheat and re-shipping the flour for consumption, with the profits of the manufacturers included, will foot up $5,000,000 per annum.

It requires a very simple arithmetical calculation to demonstrate that, by this injudicious policy, the great wheat-growing State of Texas is voluntarily submitting to a wrong of the gravest character—in fact, is permitting its subsistence to be thrown away in the most profligate manner. Our 20,000,000 bushels of wheat converted into flour at home would about meet the Texas demand, while the three-fourths now imported for consumption costs the consumers $21,000,000. Against these figures place the home value of our entire wheat product—$16,000,000—and it is an easy matter to see what a loss is sustained, irrespective of the bran, shorts and middlings, by the inconsistent method of sending this grain crop abroad to be manufactured into flour which is immediately returned, at a handsome profit to the millers, to us for consumption. It is a well known fact that the favorite brands of flour imported by us are, to a very great extent, made of Texas wheat, and no wonder, therefore, that those only partially acquainted with the true state of affairs so often ask: "Why does not Texas make her own flour?" It is because there is a lack of mills of the highest improved order, that can turn out flour of the finest quality, of the highest grades and of a sufficient capacity to manufacture the entire wheat crop grown in Texas. Can any one doubt the assertion that Austin is one of the most inviting fields in the State for capital that will establish flouring mills of this character?

ICE MANUFACTURING.

Few, if any, industrial undertakings in the South give evidence of more genuine enterprise than the manufacture of artificial ice, and few have reached greater magnitude, while absolutely none can lay claim to a more important rank as contributors to the health and comfort of the masses, as well as our material prosperity. The growth of the industry has been astonishing, but not more so than the improvements in the processes for manufacturing the artificial article, by which it is not only the equal of Nature's own congealment, but for some purposes it is superior to the latter, while as a rival upon the score of cost, its extremely low price to consumers enables all to enjoy its benefits, thus making it an invaluable boon to the South, where in former days Northern ice was indeed a luxury that but very few could indulge in, and an enormous expense under circumstances where the consumption of very large quantities was an unavoidable necessity.

There are two ice manufactories in Austin, with a combined capacity of about twenty-five tons per day, which is ample at present to supply the entire local demand and a very profitable trade from the surrounding country. The trade from abroad, however, is expanding so rapidly that a very considerable increase of capacity is contemplated at an early day by our manufacturers, and which fact is the most substantial evidence that could be adduced, as to the superior quality and cheapness of the ice they turn out.

LEATHER INTERESTS.

There is no possible reason to be offered why Austin should not be one of the most advantageous sites in Texas for either the manufacture of leather, or any of the various industries in which that material is used as the chief factor. Hides, which like "Topsey," who said "she jist growed," sprung up spontaneously all over the State, apparently without any effort on the part of anyone, being the production of an industry which stands side by side with agriculture, and which, notwithstanding its mammoth proportions, is conducted at such a minimum of cost, that if the yield of beef alone was the only part of cattle that could be utilized, still the raising of them would remain the same lucrative industry in Texas. Besides the enormous quantity of hides sent out of the State annually on the live cattle we ship, there are also 30,000,000 pounds of hides prepared for the tanner within the State. But unfortunately, and to our shame it must be confessed, their further development ceases at that point, for the 30,000,000 pounds of hides are sent abroad to be manufactured into leather, and the leather to be manufactured into boots and shoes, harness and saddlery and many other commodities, which are then sent to us for consumption. The enormous loss entailed upon Texas by this injudicious management in the years gone by has reached a sum, the magnitude of which would scarcely be credited were it possible to compute it in exact dollars and cents. But vast as is the loss consequent upon the shipment of our hides cured at home to Northern manufactures, how incomparably greater must be the sum total of our losses upon hides through the immense shipments of live cattle abroad.

There was a time when, how to prevent this vast loss upon the hides produced in Texas, was a problem too difficult of solution to be given serious consideration, but it is no longer so. With the establishment of large tanneries and the erection of boot and shoe factories thoroughly equipped with capital, improved labor-saving machinery and spirited enterprise, throughout the State, and this constant drifting of the raw material in the form of hides to Northern manufacturers, will speedily grow visibly less, and it will cease *entirely* when our cattlemen wake up to the importance of slaughtering at home and shipping dressed beeves in refrigerator cars to the great markets abroad. When this work of reform has been fully accomplished, Texas will no longer be deprived of the profits on commodities that can be produced here cheaper than in any other State in the Union, and therefore enabling our manufacturers to give home consumers the advantage of lower prices, and the very best grade of goods, without cutting profits under those enjoyed by the manufacturers North, who are now supplying our wants in these respects.

It is only a question of time (and its speedy coming is now more strongly indicated than ever before), when this flattering condition of affairs for the leather interests will prevail all over the State, and in no section is there more promising advantages for ripe development than the city of Austin possesses. The various industries represented in the class of manufactures depending on leather as the chief of raw materials are becoming firmly established here, and those already founded are paving the way for other accessions equally as energetic, by their commendable enterprise and vigorous growth. First in these several lines of manufacture is

TANNING,

and to which branch the rank of precedence must be given, as upon it all the others are naturally dependent. The one tannery in the city has proved itself a worthy pioneer of the industry at Austin, having by its pluck and enterprise considerably augmented the manufacturing importance and material wealth of this point. The product is, of course, limited to a very ordinary extent, as the demand for Texas-made leather has not yet become so general among the auxiliary branches of the industry as to make the home article a formidable rival of the imported makes. However, the output of our tannery will stand the most critical examination of its qualities, and in this respect and in the cost to consumers, it acknowledges no superior, and the popular favor it is creating shows that its merits will soon make it a competitor that will lead in the home markets and secure it a conspicuous place in those abroad.

BOOT AND SHOE

manufacturing, though confined principally to custom orders, has begun to branch out to manufacturing for the trade. And though the operations are conducted upon only a small scale, the enterprise thus exhibited recommends it to the highest consideration by the public, as it will eventually secure the fullest recognition through Austin's development as one of the prominent boot and shoe manufacturing centers of Texas. It is difficult to conceive of a line of industry that could be established by large capital in Austin with the assurance of more positive success than the manufacture of boots and shoes. The facilities for obtaining raw material are equal to those at *any other point in the State*. The territory tributary to the trade of the city is of an extent and char-

acter that guarantees the most liberal support, and the advantages for obtaining a market for the product outside of this natural home trade, are fully up
to the standard of those found elsewhere. The cost of conducting the manufacture here can be reduced to the minimum by judicious management without difficulty, while the attractive surroundings for operatives, in the way of
cheap food supplies, cheap fuel, cheap rents, and a pleasant, healthy home in
the most beautiful city in the State, renders it an easy matter to secure and
retain the most competent of skilled labor. More inviting inducement than
these cannot be held out by any other city in the State claiming to be a
natural manufacturing point, and so favorable a combination of advantages
cannot fail of influence in securing to the Capital City the most beneficial
results.

SADDLERY AND HARNESS.

The manufacture of saddlery and harness is a line of industry which
receives very liberal encouragement indeed in Texas, for no State in the Union
is a greater consumer of such articles. And though Northern made goods are
extensively sold in the State, the trade in this class of commodities is one of
the very few which finds in the home manufactures the leading competitor,
especially such goods as properly come within the definition of the term, saddlery. It is a strange fact, that almost every State in the Union—and we may
also say with truth, every country in the world—has adopted some particular
style of saddle and other horse accoutrements, and for which the attachment
is so strong that it is difficult to find a parallel outside of the prejudice in favor
of the costumes peculiar to the various nations of the earth. Why this feature
in horse apparel should have reached such an extreme as to become so very
remarkable in the several sections of one common country like ours, is a conun-
drum which we cannot afford to waste time upon in the attempt to solve.
We know that such is a fact, and those who are posted on Texas eccentricities,
knows how particular a Texan is in the selection of a saddle, a bridle, a girth
or a bit, or *any part* of the outfit for the animal so commonly used as a medium
of conveyance; and no manufacturer can suit the native fancy so thoroughly
as our home manufacturers who are perfectly familiar with the peculiarities in
this direction.

The success which Austin has made as a manufacturer of this line of
goods, is of the most substantial character, and it is doubtful if the products of
any other point in Texas can compete with those turned out here, either in the
home market or abroad. As an evidence of this fact and also of the magnitude of the industry at Austin, one of our establishments alone does a business
to the amount of half a million dollars per annum, having branches in no less
than six of the most prominent points in the State, and commanding a trade
that reaches throughout Texas, Arkansas, Louisiana, Mississippi, and extends

even into Tennessee. An exhibit like this is the most fitting praise that could
be expressed concerning the able character of Austin as a manufacturer of harness and saddlery.

HORSE COLLAR

manufacturing is also conducted in the city as a distinct line of industry, and
constitutes one of our most progressive enterprises, well worthy of the success
being met with.

SADDLETREE MANUFACTURING,

which is closely identified with the saddlery industry, also deserves mention as
a valuable contributor to Austin's material prosperity and importance as a
center of manufactures.

WOOD-WORKING INDUSTRIES.

Austin's advantages for manufacturing pursuits are well testified by the
number of various industries properly classed under this heading. The facilities at this point for obtaining the raw material, as we have already shown in
the chapter devoted to the material resources of the city, are, strictly speaking,
as favorable as those possessed by any city or town in the State. Lumber of
every description, both hard and soft varieties, is produced in abundance at our
very doors, barring pine, and that is so readily accessible that it may as well be
included in the exhaustive catalogue of wood material which the manufacturer finds here for utilization ; and, moreover, the cost of the raw material
laid down in the city is as cheap as it can be obtained at any other point in the
State adapted to general manufacturing.

Among the many pursuits dependent upon this material, none have
obtained a more important rank than the manufacture of

SASH, DOORS AND BLINDS.

In fact this branch has become the leading wood-making industry of
America, and each year sees it develop to more gigantic proportions. Austin
has every reason to be proud of its manufactures in this line, the planing mills
turning out sash, doors and blinds, mouldings, turned and scroll work, that
cannot be excelled in any respect by the manufactories at any other point in
the country. These products are shipped throughout the region tributary to
Austin in large quantities and the prominent growth of the business indicates
a future in which the city will be unusually conspicuous as a seat of this
important line of industry.

Numerous other wood-working branches are conducted in the city, and
considerable headway has been made towards establishing them as prominent
industries. There is rare skill and enterprise engaged in all of them and they
are steadily and surely growing to proportions that will satisfy in the fullest
the laudable ambition which now inspires the work of progress.

PRINTING AND PUBLISHING.

The multiplicity and diversified nature of Austin's industrial advantages, are illustrated in a marked way by the character and extent of its printing and publishing interests, and which deserve an unusual degree of credit for the substantial prosperity they are bringing to the city, by their enterprise and practical demonstrations of what can be done here by the manufacturing lines. They have won for the Capital City of Texas a most enviable reputation indeed among the public abroad, and through the energy, skill and business tact which backs them, are continually adding lustre to Austin's fame as a live, go-ahead city.

The extent to which this class of industry has reached is readily seen in the fact that

TEN NEWSPAPERS

and periodicals are now published in the city, although its population still numbers less than 20,000. While it is true that these publications do not rely solely upon the Austin public for support—for printed matter, edited and published here goes regularly to thousands of readers scattered in every city and town in the United States—still, here was their birth-place, it was Austin that fostered and encouraged them, giving them their first prestige, and to Austin they continue to look for the approbation that insures future success.

THE STATESMAN

is the leading daily journal, being issued every morning except Monday, with a weekly edition appearing every Thursday. The Statesman was established in 1871, and was first issued as a twenty column tri-weekly. It has steadily grown in size—and also in popularity—to a thirty-six column daily, and through the ability and enterprise in its editorial and managerial departments is now generally recognized as the leading democratic paper of the Southwest.

THE DISPATCH

represents the republican side of politics, and is issued every evening except Sunday. It is a bright, energetic journal that reflects credit alike upon the liberal spirit of the community and the genuine newspaper skill of the staff in control.

TEXAS SIFTINGS

is known *everywhere* and highly appreciated by its vast number of readers who are found in every section of this country and many English speaking communities of Europe. It is a weekly, issued every Saturday, and is independent in politics, invading every field of life with its free lance of humor. Its career has been as phenomenal as the spirit of dash which prompted the establishment of such a journal in this extreme part of the South, is remarkable. No paper of a similar character outside of New York has ever had a like success, and none have attained a wider circulation.

THE AUSTIN WOCHENBLATT

is a weekly issue, devoted to the German interests of the State at large and the general prosperity of Austin in particular. Judicious management and the sterling ability of the editorial corps has established it upon a substantial basis and given it a prominent rank among the most popular German papers in the State.

The remaining publications are as follows:

Texas Farm and Ranch.—A semi-monthly journal devoted to the agricultural and pastoral interests of the State, which circulates extensively throughout the South and Southwest.

Texas State Journal.—A monthly issue representing land and railway interests.

Texas Baptist Herald.—A weekly, and the standard organ of the Baptist order of religion in the State.

The Homœopathic Pellet is a medical journal published monthly; and The Texian (a monthly), and The American Sketch Book (issued in numbers irregularly), are devoted to social interests.

The diversified character of these publications and the eminent success they are enjoying, testify no less to the intelligence and social refinement of Austin, than to its progressiveness, as a business and industrial point.

The facilities of Austin in every branch of the printing and publishing business are unsurpassed in the Southwest, and the equipments for rapid and fine work are upon the whole *better* perhaps than is possessed at any other point in the State, while the work turned out cannot be excelled in any city of the Union.

A number of other industries have been established in the city, which are steadily being developed under the influence of manufacturing skill and keen business enterprise, to substantial proportions that will eventually rank them with any of a like kind in the State, and it is reasonable to believe they will become the peers of any in the country. But there is no need to dwell upon their characteristic features. Sufficient has been outlined to show that Austin's manufacturing interests are all progressive and prosperous, that the controlling spirits are not drones in the vineyards of labor, but active, energetic workers, ambitious to excel.

The latest statistics concerning the industrial enterprises existing in the city, shows 185 establishments of all kinds, great and small, classified as follows:

Bakeries, 6; barbers, 11; blacksmiths, wagon and carriage shops, 18; bookbinders, printers, stereotypers, etc., 6; boot and shoemakers, 11; brickmakers, 2; cabinetmakers, 3; candy manufacturers, 2; contractors, carpenters and builders, 14; dyeing and scouring, 1; florists, 3; flouring mills, 2; foundries and machine shops, 4; gas companies, 2; gas-fitters and plumbers, 5; gun and locksmithing, 3; hair goods, 2; horse collar manufacturing, 1; ice factories, 2; jewelry and watchmaking, 6; laundries, 4; lime manufacturers, 2; lumber, doors, sash and blinds, 6; mattress manufacturers, 2; marble yards, 3; meat markets, 14; milliners, 9; newspapers, 10; omnibus, dray and transfer lines, 5; painters, 8; photographers, 4; saddlery and harness manufacturing, 4; safe manufacturing, 1; soap manufacturing, 1; soda water manufacturing, 1; tailors, 6; telegraph and telephone companies, 1; water works 1; total, 185.

These various industries give employment to about 1,300 people—exclusive of the clerical force they also support—among whom nearly $1,000,000 per annum are disbursed, while the total value of the products will reach to fully $5,000,000, an increase of fifty per cent. during the past three years.

This very handsome showing of our industrial enterprise at this stage in the development of Austin's advantages, is an unqualified tribute of praise to the high order of skill, executive ability and sagacious judgment—and the push and pluck as well—which has come into our midst full of confidence in the city's possibilities, to labor in the fruition of Nature's designs concerning the Capital of Texas—to build up its greatness as a seat of manufacturing industries. The record thus far is a bright one that may be accepted as a true indication of what the future will reveal, yet it but faintly foreshadows the illimitable prosperity in store for us, if the golden opportunity is properly handled, and the vast wealth of resources at the city's command thoroughly utilized by the vigorous hand of capital.

An immense number of the most useful, and also the most profitable, industries are yet to be introduced in the city, although the inducements it holds out to them to come and partake of its bounty are of the most substantial and liberal nature, and *cannot* be excelled elsewhere. The immense water power of the Colorado River is patiently waiting to set in motion any number of great mills that may levy tribute upon its lasting capacities. Is it not specially inviting as a site for

COTTON MILLS?

With this cheap power at our hand, the fleecy staple springing up, like magic, in abundance upon every side, and skilled labor easy to be obtained, capital ought to make Austin resound with the busy hum of thousands of spindles. Nothing has yet been developed to show that Southern cotton mills cannot do well when there is a profitable sale for cotton goods. On the contrary, it has been substantially demonstrated that the manufacturing can be *just as well* and *more cheaply* done near to the staple. But, while admitting this fact, capital interposes as an objection to the further increase of milling capacity in the South, the large number of factories now idle or running on short time in both the North and the South; the depressed condition of the market from over-production, and the necessity for Congress to first regulate the tariff question. As an answer to such arguments, let there be more enterprise exhibited by our cotton mills—let our manufacturers push out for themselves and *find* markets, instead of sitting apathetically in a cushioned armchair waiting for Congress to open the way. A fair sample of the lively "rustling" kind of enterprise just now needed in the cotton industries throughout the country is shown by the Libby Cotton Mills at Augusta, Ga., which are filling orders for their product from Manchester, England. Let this example of spirited progress be followed, even if it is necessary to "hustle" in the antipodes for trade, and mills everywhere will soon be making full time and the cry of over-production will cease to be the bugbear of the present gigantic proportions.

Again, let there be a decided improvement in the grades of goods made. It is the coarser grades of cloth that have become a glut on the home market and for which it is equally difficult to find a foreign sale. Notwithstanding the United States is the greatest cotton producing country in the world, and the mournful cry is heard ascending on every hand that the over-production by our cotton mills is bringing destitution in the land, yet it is a naked fact that our imports of cotton manufacturers are still *three times* greater than our exports. All this excess, however (and to the shame of our superior manufacturing skill it must be said), consists of fancy goods, the domestic manufacture of which has not yet reached that perfection towards which, we may congratulate ourselves, it is tending, but so slowly that we may expect that, for some years to come, we will have to draw upon Europe for more or less of this class of goods to supply that demand which the home manufactures will be unable to meet. And to bear us out in these assertions, we introduce the following statement showing the imports and exports of cotton manufactures into and from the United States during the census year of 1880:

	Imports.	Exports.
Piece goods, plain	$5,835,000	$1,020,000
Piece goods, printed	1,180,000	2,956,000
Hosiery, shirts, etc	7,515,000	....
Jeans, denims	1,068,000	....
All other manufactures	19,146,000	1,190,000
Total	$34,744,000	$5,166,000

Very clearly the work of radical reform must be prosecuted most vigorously within our mills before they can look for a full share of prosperity; and it is no less apparent that factories established at Austin upon the most improved systems for turning out products to meet the demands of the day, will become a practical success of the highest order.

Another manufacturing industry which is of the greatest importance to the country in general and the State of Texas in particular, for which Austin is peculiarly fitted to become a thriving seat of, is the manufacture of

WOOLEN MATERIALS.

The same sterling advantages which cordially invites the founding of cotton factories at this point, holds out the same special inducements to this natural associate interest. The production of wool is comparatively a new, but rapidly growing, industry in Texas, the present yield being about 30,000,000 pounds per annum. The cost of transportation on the crop, however, exceeds cotton in proportion to the yield, and the manufacturers' profits are correspondingly greater. Hence, when we consider the decided advantages in favor of manufacturing our wool crop at home, the fact that we have but two woolen mills in the State, and the thorough adaptability of Austin as a center for the manufacture of woolen goods, it is not only obvious that the most satisfying outcome would result from the establishment of such plants here, but there is every reason to believe that the industry could be built up to a degree of magnitude that would excel all others located in our midst.

With the development of cotton and wool manufactures, there would naturally spring a multitude of auxiliary manufactures to the great benefit of the two principal industries, and the material advancement of the public prosperity. Indeed, with these great textile industries firmly established in the city, the diversified manufactures which will speedily follow, and the character, extent and value of the products, will rapidly develop Austin as the "Lowell" of the South. And it can be made the prototype of Holyoke by the introduction of

PAPER MILLS.

Nowhere within the broad expanse of the great State of Texas, with its countless advantages for the important manufacture of paper, is there to be found a single mill, and as a consequence the point which first exhibits its enterprise by founding the industry, will enjoy pre-eminence for all time to come in the manufacture, as well as a complete monopoly for years hence. Austin has the water power to turn the wheels of not one, but several such mills, and the raw material in the form of rags can be obtained here as readily, and as cheap, as at any of the great paper making towns of Massachusetts or elsewhere, while the wood pulp which now enters so largely into its manufacture, and also the vegetable substances, indigenous to Mexico and parts of Texas in the same latitudes, which have in recent years been pronounced by science as peculiarly fitted for making paper, are in such abundance, that naught but capitalized enterprise is required to make the city, *the* paper manufacturing center of the South and the peer of *any* in the entire country.

But lack of space forbids the further enumeration of the productive interests that can be established here with the positive assurance of rapidly developing a superlative degree of success. Suffice that Austin has been fully endowed by Nature with every pre-requisite essential to the full maturing of every line of industry coming within the entire range of human skill and enterprise, and it remains for man alone to take hold of these advantages and make the city a vast aggregation of talent, capital, mechanical comprehensiveness and immense resources of construction and production. The task has been undertaken, and considerable headway upon the noble work has been made by the brave hearts now engaged on it, but a greater force is necessary to complete it in all its fullness and perfect symmetry of design. Will fresh spirits and vigorous hands, armed with new enterprises, come into the field to assist in the accomplishing the grand results? The reward is great, and the Capital City of Texas says in cordial tones to one and all alike, come! and share in the bounty of my harvest.

Before closing that portion of our work devoted to the advantages of Austin as a great seat of commerce and manufactures, it is incumbent upon us to give, at least, a brief notice of that class of intersts which by their vigorous aid in advancing business enterprises and promoting the general prosperity of the city, have become factors in its development too important to be ignored under any circumstances. We allude to that class in which are found consolidated the higher order of executive ability, financial skill and capital, for the purpose of facilitating and expediting by specific ways and means, business affairs of every description and the building up and improving of all the various interests essential in the betterment of a great community, as for instance,

BANKS AND BANKERS.

Austin now has three national banks and two private banking houses, namely; First National Bank, incorporated in 1872; State National Bank, organized as the successor of Bremond & Co., private bankers, in 1882, with a capital of $100,000; City National Bank, organized during the past year as successor to the private banking house of A. P. Wooldrige, and capitalized to the amount of $100,000, and J. H. Raymond & Co. and Foster & Co., German-American Bank.

These banking institutions represent an ample capital to facilitate the movements of trade and commerce, and by their judicious management and sound integrity have secured a well deserved reputation in financial circles throughout the country.

The principal other corporations that are of special benefit to the city's progress, are as follows:

Austin Savings' and Loan Association.   Incorporated May 9, 1883.

Austin Board of Underwriters.   Organized May, 1872.

Austin City Railroad.   Chartered 1873.   Capital stock, $50,000.   (The principal line of this street railway extends from Union depot, on Congress Avenue to city park, a distance of two miles).

Austin Telephone Exchange.

Austin Gas-light and Coal Company.   Organized 1875.

Capital Gas-light Company.   Chartered 1883.

City Water Company.   Incorporated 1875.

Capital State Fair Association.   Organized March 26, 1875.

Texas Building Association.   Organized December, 1878.

Travis County Road and Bridge Company.   (The magnificent iron bridge spanning the Colorado River at the foot of Congress Avenue and erected under the supervision of this corporation, constitutes the finest specimen of bridge architecture south of St. Louis.   It is of the high truss pattern, having an extreme length of 910 feet).

Southwestern Telegraph and Telephone Company, and two express companies—the Pacific Express and the Texas Express.

There are also quite a number of benevolent and social organizations in the city, to which allusion will be made in the closing pages of this work, confined more strictly to those features which have served to spread abroad, to such a remarkable extent, Austin's fame as a

RESIDENCE CITY,

and to which subject we now invite the reader's attention.

Austin's reputation as the most beautiful city in Texas is in nowise an exaggeration of the truth.   Viewed from the hills south of the Colorado River, its appearance is one of grandeur as the eye rests first upon the most prominent features—the sublime surroundings of Nature's handiwork, making doubly conspicuous that of man in the magnificent buildings which adorns the site.   Yet as the gaze takes in the whole of the scene—the landscape diversified by rugged mountains, broad valleys, high undulating prairies, cultivated fields and primeval forests, extending far beyond and to the right and left of Capitol hill; the ornate public edifices, elegant private residences, the less pretentious dwellings and neat cottages, built upon the succession of rock-crowned hills overlooking the clear waters of the Colorado—there is found such simplicity and perfect harmony in its completeness as to make it a singularly picturesque sight that never fails to elicit the highest admiration.

But these charms are made even more attractive by an acquaintance with the delightful

CLIMATE,

which is mild and equable the year round, strongly suggestive of that of

Southern France and Italy. The atmosphere combines much of the softness of that of the gulf coast, without its humidity, with the salubrity of the elevated plains of the northwestern section of the State. The extreme oppressiveness of summer so common in more northern latitudes, is almost unknown here. Indeed to such an extent is the climate modified by the prevailing southerly breezes from the gulf that the absolute heat, as registered by the thermometer —which, however, rarely reaches 100 degrees Fahrenheit—is not a true measure of the sensible heat in this locality. These balmy breezes from the South temper the winter's cold as well. The only severity of weather felt in winter to any great extent, is that occasioned by the sudden blasts from the regions of snow during that season, called "Northers." But these rarely exceed three days in duration, and are only considered trying in exposed places on the open plains, and even there, are not more so, except by contrast with the prevailing mild temperature, than the winter storms of higher latitudes.

The meteorological records of the late Dr. D. W. C. Baker (for many years signal observer at Austin), covering a period of twenty-five years, furnishes some interesting facts as well as reliable information concerning the character of our climate. These records show a total rainfall during twenty-five years, from 1858 to 1882 inclusive, of 231.55 inches, being an annual average of 33.26 inches. Though there were some exceptions to the rule, September ranked as the wettest month and December as the dryest. The largest amount of rain in any one month during the twenty-five years, was 13.84 inches in September, 1874. The largest amount which fell in any one shower, was seven inches in four hours, in August, 1860.

The records also show that in July, 1860, had the hottest day that occurred during the twenty-five years, the thermometer registering 107 degrees. The coldest day was in January, 1864, six degrees above zero. The thermometer only reached 100 degrees in six years out of the twenty—between 1862 and 1882; and never went lower than ten degrees above zero during the twenty-five years, except on the occasion mentioned as the coldest day. The average annual temperature during the quarter of a century thus placed on record, was 67.59 degrees.

The city is regularly and handsomely built, almost exclusively of the fine limestone found in the adjacent hills in inexhaustable quantities. The blocks are laid out with the mathematical precision of checkerboard squares, except in the newer additions where the irregularity is more in consequent with latter day progress, and acts as a relief for the Quaker-like primness of the older portion of the city. Its broad, handsome thoroughfares are well paved with durable stone, and present a neat, clean appearance at all times, the natural system of drainage, by reason of the favorable topographical features, being very thorough. The street nomenclature adopted by the founders of the city, have been rigidly adhered to, as it embodied originality and good judgment, and is pleasing to the taste and pride of the country. The names of streets running north and south, with the exception of Congress Avenue, are for Texas streams, and those running east and west for the trees indigenous to Texas. Rare common sense is also displayed in house numbering, one hundred numbers being allowed to each block, regardless of the number of lots or houses it contains. On streets running north and south, the river is the initial point, the numbers extending northward therefrom, the even numbers being placed on the west side and the odd ones on the east side, while on those streets running east and west, Congress Avenue (which leads directly up to the Capitol's main front, and is the central dividing line of the city) is the base, the numbers extending each way being the same, but prefixed by the words "east" and "west," as for instance, No. 563 East Pecan Street, and No. 563 West Pecan Street. North of Magnolia Avenue (the twentieth street north of the Colorado River), however, Wichita Street is taken for the dividing line between the east and west running numbers, instead of Congress Avenue, that portion of the city containing new additions in which, by the irregularity of platting, Wichita Street is the central line. The even numbers are placed on the north side, and the odd ones on the south side of the east and west bound street. This system of numbering is the simplest that could be devised and the stranger experiences little or no difficulty in finding the locality of any particular street and house number in the city.

Austin is fully abreast of all other cities in Texas, and the majority of the greater ones of the country, in the way of internal improvements of the advanced order of the day. The admirably arranged system of water works furnishes an ample supply of pure water, brought from the clear running Colorado at a distance sufficiently removed to be beyond all danger of contamination by the encroachments of civilization for years to come; and even when that period arrives, the inexhaustible source of supply is susceptible of improvements that will meet every requirement of the future age.

The city is well lighted with gas, there being two well established companies, the competition between which insures the municipality and the public generally, a plentiful supply of excellent gas at cheap rates.

The steam, fire and the police departments are thoroughly systematized and efficient, affording reliable protection from fire and crime.

EDUCATIONAL FEATURES.

The proper facilities for education are always to be regarded as preeminent among the most important advantages necessary in advancing the social economy of any community to the highest order of perfection. In this respect Austin has always held a leading rank among Texas cities, its educational opportunities being eminently great and continually growing more comprehensive in deference to the demands of progress.

As is pretty generally known throughout the country, Texas, by the liberal policy of law-makers since its early foundation as a Republic, has become possessed of the most magnificent public school system that is to be found in any State of the Union, it being endowed with 33,000,000 acres of land, which, together with the cash, bonds and other investments, makes the aggregate value of the permanent school fund to-day nearly $100,000,000. The interest only of this permanent fund is available for school purposes, but that a handsome income accrues therefrom is to be seen from the late report of the Department of Education, in which the available school fund for the year beginning September 1, 1885, is placed at $2,232,272. This liberal system of education is further sustained by taxation, thus preventing any deficits which might otherwise occur, and insuring to every community a thorough educational training for its children.

Austin's public schools are well disciplined by competent trustees and efficient teachers and rank as the most popular institutions of learning in our midst. The statement of their condition, as it appeared in the late report issued by the Department of Education, though by no means complete (because, as is alleged, of failure on the part of the city school authorities to send in the statistics in full to the Department), is nevertheless important in showing to a partial extent, at least, the growth and value of the system here. We give the report thus furnished for the last two scholastic years, 1882–83, and 1883–84, as follows:

Scholastic Year.	No. Schools.			No. Pupils Enrolled.			Average School Term.	Scholastic Population reported by Assessors.			State Apportionment.	Paid Teachers, etc., by City.
	White.	Colored.	Total.	White.	Colored.	Total.	Months.	White.	Colored.	Total.	Amount.	Amount.
1882–83.........	21	6	27	....	....	....	9 7-20	904	555	1,459	$5,278	$8,623 05
1883–84.........	26	8	34	1,224	560	1,784	8 14-20	1,016	594	1,610	7,245	....

UNIVERSITY OF TEXAS.

The superior facilities for education afforded by the Texas public school system in the ordinary course, embracing the primary, grammar and high school grades, are supplemented by a collegiate course in the University of Texas, which institution—the crowning glory of our common school system—very properly was located at the Capital City. This magnificent institute of higher learning, designed to be the peer of any in the whole land in magnitude and thoroughness of capacity for educational training, as it is now the

equal in point of munificence of endowment, was first opened for the matricu-
lation of students September 15, 1883. Its benefits are free to all who desire
to avail themselves of its advantages—male and female alike—barring the
colored race, for whom, however, a branch institute fully the equal in every
respect, is to be erected, measures for its early erection having already been
adopted.

The University grounds are situated on College Hill, a beautiful eminence
just north of Capitol Hill, between San Marcos and Lampasas Streets. This
healthy site, shaded with cedar, is strikingly grand, while the surrounding
landscape, as viewed from the upper windows of the University building,
almost surpasses description, so peculiarly harmonious are the blendings of its
seemingly ever-changing scenes replete with varied charms. The endowment
of the University consists of 1,219,900 acres of the public domain, and cash,
land notes and State bonds amounting to $523,156.30 (according to the last
annual report of the Treasurer of the State), which constitutes a permanent
fund. The annual resources of the University, arising from the rental of its
lands and the interest on its invested securities, approximates now about
$85,000. This income, however handsome though it is, is not sufficient to
complete the entire designs of the University and support it as an institution
of the highest educational standard dispensing its privileges free to the young
men and women of Texas. But it is confidently expected that the State will
promptly meet its requirements with further appropriations, in order that the
noble work thus auspiciously begun may achieve the grandest possible success.

The Agricultural and Mechanical College, located near Bryan, Brazos
County, is a branch of the University, which, in addition to its proportion of
the University fund, is endowed with $209,000 in State bonds, the proceeds of
the land grant of 180,000 acres to Texas by the United States government,
under the act of Congress authorizing the establishment and maintainance of
such colleges in the various States of the Union. Its progress as a technical
school is highly gratifying to the people, and there are flattering indications
that future development will cause it to rank among the most prominent institutions of the kind in America.

The Medical Branch of the University will be located in Galveston, that
city presenting greater advantages for clinical instruction than any other point
in the State. With these two exceptions, all other branches will be established
at Austin, the seat of the main institution.

Austin is also well supplied with private educational institutes, which are
very efficient and are liberally sustained.

RELIGIOUS

privileges are also dispensed most liberally in the Capital City, and are highly
appreciated. A score of church edifices grace the city, adding materially to its

architectural beauties, as well as contributing largely to the improvement of its moral tone. Methodist, Baptist, Presbyterian, Episcopal, Roman Catholic, Christian, Lutheran and Hebrew denominations are largely represented, and work with harmonious accord for the betterment of society. And it may be truthfully said that the society of Austin exhibits, to a marked extent, the highest type of culture, grace and intelligence. Cosmopolitan in tastes and exceedingly tolerant in spirit, the utmost cordiality prevails among all classes, inspiring the stranger at once with confidence in the genuineness of the fellowship displayed.

These characteristics are, furthermore, continually developing through the influence of the many different social and benevolent organizations existing in the city. The various orders represented embrace the Masonic order, Odd Fellows, Knights of Honor, Knights of Pythias, Legion of Honor, Ancient Order of United Workmen, Knights of Labor, B'nai Brith, Texas Veteran Association, Temperance Union, and many other fraternal organizations of high standing in every city of the Union. That the numerical strength of their membership in the aggregate is very great, is to be seen in the fact that there are upwards of fifty distinct lodges and societies in the city. Besides these civic bodies, there are three military organizations — the Austin's Grays (Infantry), Travis Light Artillery, and the Austin City Rifles (Colored Infantry).

But not the least of Austin's attractions as a residence city, are those due to the greatness thrust upon it by having been selected by the State as its

SEAT OF GOVERNMENT.

This fact alone has been sufficient to make it the center of many influences of great weight in elevating its intellectual, moral and social standard. The excitement natural from its being the political center of the State adds zest to life, and by the contrast serves to make the quiet home charms all the more delightful.

The beneficial influence upon Austin through its prominence as the Capital is especially marked in the growing interest manifested by its people in the architectural improvement of the city, and which is not more conspicuously displayed in structures for business and public purposes generally, than in residences, even of the humblest character, and the beautifying of their surroundings. This laudable ambition, which is at once a strong indication of a natural refinement, and an earnest desire to cultivate the love of the beautiful to the highest degree of excellence, is largely fostered and encouraged by the Government, which in the character and design of the

STATE BUILDINGS

already erected, and those in course of construction, and contemplated, has exhibited wise forethought and broad judgment, combined with a correct knowledge of the architectural requirements of the age, a just appreciation of the value of the advances made in the science of building on the present, and an excellent conception of the influence its progress will have on the future of the American people, that is worthy of emulation by individuals, corporations and governments in all sections of the country.

The State Institution for the Blind, the Insane Asylum, the Deaf and Dumb Asylum, the main University building, and the Central Land Office, are State edifices which reflect credit upon Texas, and are prominent among the architectural adornments of the Capital, and which, together with the Travis County Court House, and the United States Government Building (both handsome edifices of recent construction), are objects of special interest to visitors.

But the crown piece of Austin's future glory as a city of magnificent edifices, will be found in the

CAPITOL BUILDING,

now in course of erection on Capitol Hill, and upon which Texas is expending lavish wealth and every effort that architectural skill and constructive genius can contribute, to make it a fitting emblem of the greatness and grandeurs of this immense State, a monument to its wonderful progress in the first half century of its existence as a member of the Union Sisterhood, and a time-enduring evidence of American achievements in the work of higher civilization. When complete, the Texas State Capitol will have *absolutely* no peer in the entire country except the Capitol of the United States, and will rank in all respects as one of the finest structures in the world. The design, combining as it does, all the essential elements of proportion, dignity, size, adaptability, and modern improvement, is conceded by every competent judge to be a fair reflex of the enlightenment of our age.

The Commissioners' description of the building, however, will enable our readers to form a clearer conception of the splendid structure when complete, and which in substance is as follows:

"It is located on the commanding elevation, known as Capitol Hill, near the center of the city, and in the square originally selected for the capitol of the republic of Texas. The north front rests on Peach Street, facing University Hill, and the mountainous background to the left and rear; the east and west wings front on Colorado and Brazos Streets respectively, while the south, standing at right angles with Congress Avenue, and parallel with Mesquite Street, overlooking the river and the evergreen hills beyond, presents a view of surpassing beauty.

"The style of architecture is classic, with modern treatment, the outlines being sufficiently broken to give stately appearance and to secure proper contrasts of light and shade. The various combinations of scientific principle are employed to combine that simplicity, harmony and grandeur which alone is approved by cultured taste.

"The dimensions, at greatest measure, are 566½ feet long by 288 feet 10 inches wide. The building is three stories in height above the basement, besides a fourth or central story, running from the north to the south pediment.

"Of all similar structures in America, it is second in size only to the National Capitol at Washington, D. C., and is larger and finer than the German Reichstag or English Parliament buildings. The provisions for the executive, legislative and judicial departments, including educational, agricultural, geological, military, historical and other appointments, are ample and complete. The entire structure will rest on solid rock. The foundation walls will be six feet eight inches thick; those for the dome seven feet four inches thick —all to be made of dimension stone dressed, and laid in cement. The extensive system of pipes and appliances for sewerage, ventilation, steam-heating, water, gas and electricity, is embedded in the limestone beneath and enclosed in mortar.

"The basement story extends sufficiently above the grade-line to insure natural ventilation and sun-lighting. The water-table is a belt of red Texas granite, five feet deep, extending the entire circumference of the building, cut in two sections and finished with wash and ovolo, or Grecian moulding. The ashlar work is square rustic, sand-rubbed, illustrated with carved cap, mould, dentil and modillion. Massive pilasters, consisting of pedestal, band and fluted monolith, extend throughout the second and third stories, a feature at once elegant and imposing. These columns are crowned with rich Corinthian capitals, and sustain an entablature composed of architrave, frieze and cornice, appropriately embellished, and which, in turn, is surmounted with balustrade, pavillion and urn. Each of the cut stone pediments that adorn the four fronts enclose the Lone Star, made of heavy plate glass, secured in the masonry, and so ground that the light, natural or artificial will show distinctly the shape of that emblem. The iron roof truss and plan seem the perfection of mechanical engineering; while the minutiæ of construction and combination of materials —slate, cement, glass and metals—are all that could reasonably be desired.

"Towering above all is the great dome, which, with the triumphal arch over the south entrance, are the distinctive features of the design. The tholobate, or base of dome superstructure, is about 130 feet above the basement floor. At the height of 156 feet is the base of the colonnade formed around the rotunda by huge bronze columns, enclosing an open-air promenade inferior to nothing on the continent. Still above, at 180 feet, and again at the apex of the dome, around the foot of the lantern, 250 feet high, are circular balusters, securing open balconies, which are reached from the winding stairway within the cupola.

"The arrangements throughout the several stories, of departments, offices, halls, courts, libraries, corridors, business rooms, vaults, closets, elevators, stairways, railings, ceilings and pendants, are as unique as they are practical and complete. Almost all the rooms have direct sunlight during some portion of the day. Perfect ventilation is secured by mechanical process, which expels all vitiated air, and supplies the vacuum continuously with fresh currents, by means of ducts for that purpose.

"The first story contains accommodations for the Governor's office and apartments, five rooms; Secretary of State's office and apartments, five rooms; Attorney General's office and apartments, five rooms; Comptroller's office and apartments, eleven rooms; Treasurer's office and apartments, four rooms; Statistics, office and apartments, three rooms; Agriculture, office and apartments, three rooms; Education, office and apartments, three rooms; Adjutant-General's office and apartments, three rooms; Geological Department, office, three rooms; Police and Janitor's office and apartments, three rooms; Treasurer's vault and safe, one room; Secretary of State's vault, one room; Comptroller's vault, three rooms.

"All the above rooms are arranged en suite, and are relatively of proper dimensions.

"In the second story, east of the central dome is located the Senate Chamber, 72 by 76 feet, capable of conveniently accommodating 118 members. Surrounding this room are convenient cloak-rooms, lobbies and toilet-rooms. There are also in this section of the building two Lieutenant-Governor's rooms, one enrolling clerk's room, one engrossing room, twelve committee rooms and one postoffice.

"West of the central dome is located the Hall of Representatives, 76 by 96 feet, capable of accommodating about 240 members. This hall is likewise surrounded by convenient cloak-rooms, lobbies and toilet-rooms. There are also two speaker's rooms, one enrolling clerk's room and one engrossing room.

"South of the dome in the center of the building is the Governor's state room (to be used also for a portrait gallery), and north of the dome is the State library, 122 by 64 feet, which room is connected by a private stairway with the law library above.

"The third story contains the galleries of the Senate Chamber and Hall of Representatives, one Supreme Courtroom, one Appellate Courtroom (each 37 by 68 feet), one law library, 22½ by 48 feet, two court clerks' offices, nine judges' rooms, two marshal's rooms, sixteen committee rooms, one janitor's room and toilet-rooms.

"The fourth story contains nine rooms which may be advantageously used for committee rooms or for other useful purposes."

All the granite and marble, and much of the other material centering into the construction of the building, is of Texas product, and prepared for use in the State. To defray the cost of building, 3,050,000 acres of the public domain were set apart by an act of legislature, February 20, 1879. This reservation, which lies in that section of the State known as the Panhandle, the counties comprising it being as yet unorganized, was transferred to a Chicago syndicate, in consideration of the new Capitol being erected complete. The cost, it has been discovered, will greatly exceed the original calculations of these capitalists, but the work of construction is nevertheless rapidly progressing, and its early completion is assured, possibly in time for inauguration during the fiftieth anniversary year of Texas' freedom from Mexican rule.

Having briefly traced the rise and progress of Austin from an insignificant hamlet of three families only, on the very outskirts of civilization less than fifty years ago, to its present magnificent stage in which it is the Capital City of the greatest State in the Union, the seat of rare intelligence, culture and wealth, and one of the most progressive centers of trade, commerce and manufactures in the South, having unrivaled advantages for establishing its greater distinction as such in the near future, it is made clearly evident that while much of its prominence is due to the greatness thrust upon it by the people at large having declared it the permanent habitat of government, to its own citizens belongs the credit of developing the more substantial elements of its present and prospective prosperity. It is, therefore, but just and proper that the well earned meed of praise should be rendered to the energetic spirits whose industry, skill, courage and vim is utilized solely in the interest of Austin's advancement as a city capable of conferring the most desirable benefits upon mankind through its power in trade and industrial channels. The record they have made is a particularly bright one, in the delineation of which it affords great gratification to be able to devote the remaining pages of our work in behalf of the Capital City. This most interesting feature we now present to our readers under the caption of

REPRESENTATIVE BUSINESS ENTERPRISES OF AUSTIN.

P. H. GERHARD—Dealer in all Kinds of Hardware, Machinery, Etc.; 503 and 505 East Pecan Street.

This house was established six years ago, and has built up a large and lucrative trade and attained a popularity second to no similar institution in the city. The building occupied is a two story brick, with basement, well located, conveniently arranged, with elevator and other facilities for the easy

handling of goods, and covering an area of 32x128 feet. The stock carried
consists of a full line of heavy and shelf hardware, iron, barb wire, rope,
machinery and agricultural implements of all kinds, wagons, etc. The
machinery handled is of the best make and includes some of the most popular brands, and, as Mr. Gerhard deals directly with the manufacturers, he is
able to sell at factory prices, thus saving his customers many dollars in the
way of freights. He is agent for the "Old Hickory," "Luking," and "Bain"
wagon, all of which are famous for excellence of work and material, and
completeness in every respect. He makes a specialty of the Weir plow, an
implement in which are combined more good qualities than in any other one
plow made, and of which he sells large numbers every year. Mr. Gerhard
has a large trade, extending over a wide scope of territory, and aggregating
many thousands of dollars annually. He pays the closest attention to business, buying his stock carefully and judiciously, and taking advantage of
every opportunity that will enable him to offer the best goods at the lowest
prices. He is upright and liberal in all his dealings, and the uniform cour-
tesy and kindness which he extends to all who visit his establishment make
it one of the most pleasant, as well as one of the most profitable in the city
with which to establish business relations. This house is cordially recommended to our readers as worthy their most generous confidence and support.

SMITH & BRADY—Manufacturers and Dealers in Boots and Shoes;
    217 East Pecan Street.

In a review of the commercial and industrial institutions of a city, those
firms are entitled to special mention which have, from small beginnings, grown
to prominence, and whose success is due to the pluck, energy and business
capacity which have characterized their management. Among the firms of
this kind in the city, Messrs. Smith & Brady, 217 East Pecan Street, are deserving of special mention. This firm began business here nine years ago in a
small way, and by good management and thorough, progressive enterprise
they have built up a trade, extended their business, increased their stock, until
to-day, they have one of the largest and most completely stocked boot and
shoe houses in the city, and have a trade which extends throughout the city
and surrounding country, aggregating $30,000 per annum. They carry a full
and carefully selected stock of boots and shoes, embracing everything in that
line, from the finest kid slipper to the heaviest riding boot, and including the
finest brands of goods known to the trade. In the manufacturing department
are engaged a number of skillful workmen, who make to order boots and
shoes of all kinds. Messrs. B. H. Smith and W. B. Brady, who compose the
personnel of the firm, are both practical shoemakers of long experience, and
understanding the business thoroughly, they employ only first-class workmen,

and turn out nothing but first-class work. Every boot or shoe made to order
by them is warranted to fit and guaranteed to give satisfaction in every particular. The building occupied by this establishment is a two story structure,
covering an area of 23x80 feet. The lower story is used for a salesroom, and
the upper for the manufacturing department. The building is conveniently
located and well arranged for the business for which it is used. Messrs. Smith
& Brady are honest and upright business men, fair and liberal in dealing, and
are gentlemen of genial manners and courteous address. This house is cheerfully recommended to our readers as worthy their most generous confidence
and patronage.

AUSTIN GAS LIGHT AND COAL COMPANY—S. WATTS, PRES.; J. W.
PARKER, VICE-PRES.; A. E. JUDGE, SEC. AND SUPT.; E. T. EGGLESTON,
TREAS.; OFFICE AT WORKS, CORNER LIVE OAK AND COLORADO STREETS;
OFFICE OF SECRETARY, 105 LIVE OAK STREET.

It is of the first importance that the gas by which every city is lighted should
be of the best quality and made from the purest coal, and Austin may boast of
as complete a system of gas works as any city of its size in the country. Their
works are located at the corner of Live Oak and Colorado Streets, and contain
all the most improved and modern apparatus for the manufacture of gas.
Besides this, they keep on hand a large stock of coal, coke, coal tar and gas
fitting materials. It is scarcely necessary to add, that buying their coal in
immense quantities and enjoying the concessions usually given to gas companies they can put the price of gas, coke and tar at reduced rates. They are
also prepared to take contracts for gas fitting and plumbing in all its branches,
and employing only skillful and experienced workmen to guarantee satisfaction. Their officers are all gentlemen of high standing and well-known business capacity, and in their hands the interests of the company are well guarded
and advanced. All communications should be addressed to Mr. A. E. Judge,
Secretary and Superintendent, who will give them prompt attention.

A. H. ACHILLES—WHOLESALE AND RETAIL GROCERIES AND FEED; 201 WEST
PECAN STREET.

Conspicuous among the grocery establishments of the Capital City is that
of Mr. A. H. Achilles, located at 201 West Pecan Street, opposite the post office.
This gentleman carries one of the largest and finest stocks of staple and fancy
groceries, embracing all the best grades of flour, sugar, tea, coffee, spices,
canned goods, etc., that can be found in the city. He also deals in all kinds
of feed and country produce of every description, and his prices are as low as
those of any of his contemporaries. He is constantly replenishing his stock,
thus keeping it fresh at all times. Besides his large retail trade in the city, he

has an extensive wholesale trade which extends all over the entire State, and
the dealers and merchants throughout the surrounding country, who have not
formed the acquaintance of this house, will find that relations entered into with
it will prove profitable to them and of a pleasant and enduring character.
Orders from abroad receive the promptest attention and goods are delivered to
any part of the city free of charge. Mr. Achilles, the sole proprietor of this
business, is an energetic business man, prompt in all his business transactions,
and well deserves the large patronage he is receiving.

TOM MURRAH—Land and Real Estate Agent; Rooms 8 and 9, Second
    Floor, Masonic Temple.

Our real estate men are numbered by the score. Some are of many years
experience, while others are but novices in the business, and not well acquainted
with the value of property, or the practical methods to be' pursued to conduct
it properly. Mr. Murrah has for a number of years been connected with the
land and real estate business, and has a very extensive experience in this line.
His facilities for buying, selling, and exchanging real estate are unsurpassed,
and his list of property on hand is extensive and varied. His energy, accuracy
and promptness to his patrons' interests has eminently qualified him to do
justice to those who entrust their business to his care. He devotes his personal
attention to all business transactions, a feature to which he is largely indebted
for his present success. In depicting the leading representatives of each
branch of industry, it affords us no little pleasure to mention the well-known
house of Tom Murrah. The readers of this volume abroad having real estate
interests in Austin, or desirous of investment, should not fail to take advantage
of the extensive experience of this establishment.

CARL MAYER—Jeweler; 612 Congress Avenue.

Among the most attractive mercantile establishments of our principal
business thoroughfares, those devoted to the display of the various articles for
utility and ornament embraced in the comprehensive classification of jewelry,
undoubtedly claim precedence, appealing as they do to refined taste and
æsthetic instincts of all classes of the community. One of the largest and
most favorably known emporiums of this class in the city of Austin is that
of Mr. Carl Mayer, located on Congress Avenue, where, in a commodious and
handsomely arranged salesroom, are displayed, in almost bewildering profu-
sion, imported and American watches, elegant clocks, diamonds and precious
stones in a variety of settings, spectacles, eye-glasses, opera glasses, dentistry
goods, silver and plated ware, and fine jewelry of every description of modern
and fashionable styles and designs. This house was established about seven
years ago, and each succeeding year has witnessed a gratifying increase to its

trade, and to-day it ranks as one of the finest establishments in the State. Special attention is devoted to repairing watches by skilled workmen thoroughly familiar with the delicate mechanism of the various manufactures of Europe and America, and to repairing fine jewelry in the most thorough and workmanly manner. Mr. Carl Mayer, the present proprietor, is a skillful workman himself, and by a lifetime experience has acquired a thorough knowledge of the business. In conclusion, we will state that the facilities enjoyed by this house enable it to favorably compete with other contemporary concerns, both in price and quality; and those interested will find it to their advantage and profit to enter into business relations with the house of Carl Mayer.

R. L. BROWN—INVESTING AGENT.

Mr. Brown commenced here in 1883, and since establishing himself has done a large and constantly increasing business which extends throughout the city and State, amounting last year to several hundred thousand dollars. Mr. Brown is prepared to make loans to any amount, and combines with this the law and conveyance business in all its branches. He is a gentleman well-known in Austin, and is by long experience well fitted for his present business. All information regarding his business is cheerfully given, and parties here and elsewhere will find it to their advantage to call on him.

AVENUE HOTEL—CONGRESS AVENUE, LARGEST, BEST AND MOST CENTRAL HOTEL IN THE CITY; D. M. WILSON, PROPRIETOR.

Undoubtedly the most comfortable, homelike, and best fitted out hotel in Austin is the well known "Avenue Hotel" whose name heads our article. This hotel has been in existence for 25 years; and during that time has always been the favorite resort of travelers coming to Austin. Its appointments are in every respect first-class, including all the modern improvements, such as electric bells, annunciators, bathrooms, billiard tables, and restaurant, and the entire building is illuminated by electric light. There also are sample rooms for commercial travelers. From 125 to 150 guests can be accommodated without crowding. The table is spread with only the best that the market affords; and the kitchen is under the special charge of one of the best cooks in the State. The admirable location and reasonable terms of the "Avenue Hotel" render it altogether one of the most desirable stopping places in Texas. Mr. D. M. Wilson, who has recently assumed charge, is a gentleman well known in business and social circles; and has had an extensive experience as a caterer to the public. Under his efficient management, the "Avenue Hotel" will, no doubt, sustain and increase its already well established reputation as one of the best hotels in the Capital City, or the State of Texas.

AUSTIN ICE FACTORY—Joe Brunet, Proprietor.

The above house was established in 1869, and has ever since done a flourishing business. Located in a large commodious building near the Houston & Texas Central Railroad, with ample facilities and a large number of efficient hands. His daily capacity is now seventeen tons and will probably be increased the coming season. His trade is mostly located in the city, but he is ready at all times to send supplies abroad. Three engines, two of 40 and one of 50 horse-power; and one 150 horse-power boiler, and three ice machines are employed in the manufacture of this ice, the latter being of the most approved patterns. Mr. Brunet's son assists him in carrying on this enterprise, and he is perfectly familiar with the business having had a life-experience at it. It richly deserves the success it has met with, and is an institution of which the city may feel proud. The reputation of this house in the trade for enterprise and liberality is not excelled by any contemporaneous concern, while the resources and facilities at the command of the proprietor makes it one of the most desirable houses in the State with which to establish pleasant and profitable relations.

SWINDELLS' PRINTING HOUSE—1004 Congress Avenue.

Great progress has been made in the artistic branches of printing in the last decade, creating a demand for fine commercial work, and calling into existence new establishments and the latest improved machinery. The establishment of Mr. Swindells is one of the largest of this kind in the Southwest, and from his able management and superior finish and style of work has taken a leading position and an increasing trade which requires at the present time about 25 skilled workmen to keep pace with the liberal orders received. He has ample steam power to facilitate his business, and is noted not only for fine artistic work, but promptness in execution. He does all kinds of book, job, commercial work, etc., and a specialty is made of school catalogues, price lists and lawyers' briefs. He is also contractor for the State printing. Our commercial men from abroad, as well as our own city, will find this one of the best houses in the South, in which to have work done in the most expeditious and reliable manner, and last, but not least, at the lowest possible rates.

S. B. HILL—Photography; 818 Congress Avenue.

This is one of the largest art galleries in Austin. Mr. Hill, the proprietor, is a careful business man, always employing, when needed, none but thorough and practical artists. He is a careful observer, watching closely every new invention placed before the public pertaining to photography, and which, if it proves to be of any benefit to the art, is adopted. He is very favorably located at No. 818 Congress Avenue, being right in the center of the business portion of the city. His rooms are all well lighted and arranged, and his gallery is replete with all the modern appliances, and in appearance cannot be surpassed in the city. A speciality is made of copying and enlarging old pictures, and finishing in India ink, crayon, etc., and no work is allowed to leave this establishment unless it gives perfect satisfaction. We commend this house to the trade, not only on account of its superior quality of output, but for the method, liberality and fair dealings, upon which its business is conducted, and which is sure to result in pleasant and profitable relations to those who command its services.

HENRY MARTIN—Dealer in Stoves, Tinware, Table and Pocket Cutlery, etc.; 413 East Pecan Street.

Among the establishments in the city dealing in stoves, tinware, etc., the house of Henry Martin, 413 East Pecan Street, is entitled to special mention, both by reason of the size and quality of the stock carried, and because of the energy, enterprise and activity of its management. This establishment was founded about two years ago by Messrs. Grove & Martin, the latter-named gentleman buying out his partner a few months ago, and now being sole proprietor. The store occupied is centrally located and well arranged, and covers an area of 22x140 feet. The stock carried embraces a full and complete line of cook and heating stoves, tinware, table and pocket cutlery, etc., embracing some of the best and most popular brands of goods known to the market. A manufacturing department is run in connection with this establishment, in which all kinds of tin and sheet-iron work is done; and Mr. Martin being himself a practical tinner, and giving the work his close personal supervision, all the work done is first-class, and guaranteed to give satisfaction in every particular. Any of our readers who desire to purchase articles in this line should call on Mr. Martin, as an examination of his stock and prices will serve to convince them that he sells the best goods at the lowest prices, and that nowhere in the city can a house be found with which business can be transacted more pleasantly or more profitably.

JOHN SHEEHAN—Dealer in Plain and Fancy Groceries; 413 Congress Avenue.

The handsomest and best equipped family grocery in the city of Austin is that of John Sheehan, 413 Congress Avenue. Mr. Sheehan has been in the grocery business here five years, and during that time has established a reputation and built up a trade of which a much older institution might well be proud. The building he occupies is well situated, handsomely fitted up and conveniently arranged for his business, and his stock is kept in the best possible order. This stock embraces a full and complete line of plain and fancy groceries, flours, meats, provisions, coffees, teas, sugars, syrups, spices, canned goods, etc., including some of the best and most popular brands known to the trade. The large trade of this house makes the frequent receipt of new goods imperative, and thus the stock is always kept fresh, and nowhere in the city can the housekeeper find more desirable articles for table use than here. The low prices, free delivery, and polite attention bestowed upon all customers, add to the prosperity of the house and attach to it a large number of permanent patrons. Mr. Sheehan is a native of Virginia, but was raised in Texas. He is a good business man, enterprising and progressive in all his undertakings, and a gentleman of genial manners and courteous address. His establishment is cordially recommended to our readers as in every way worthy their confidence and patronage.

CAPITAL ICE FACTORY—MATTINGLEY & ZIMPELMAN, PROPRIETORS; 101 WEST WATER STREET.

Among the valuable enterprises of the past decade, and one that has brought comfort to our people, as well as been beneficial to those who have been sick is the ice factory of Messrs. Mattingley & Zimpelman, located near Congress Avenue, on Water street. The enterprise was started by Mr. Zimpelman's father about ten years ago and during the past three years it has been conducted by these young and enterprising men, who have provided the best modern machinery to facilitate the business, and can now turn out 45,000 pounds of *pure ice* per day, for which they find an increasing trade annually, now reaching most of the prominent towns and cities around Austin. From twelve to fifteen hands find employment here and their pay roll reaches about $900 monthly. Those who peruse this work can depend on getting pure ice and satisfaction in business transactions when dealing with this reliable firm. They are public spirited men and readily aid all enterprises that are of a public nature. We are glad to find space in the business history of Austin for so laudable an industry and one of so much interest to lovers of comforts of life.

JOSEPH SPENCE—REAL ESTATE AND COLLECTING AGENT; ROOM No. 1, HANCOCK BUILDING, NEXT TO POSTOFFICE.

Among the real estate firms of Austin who have for years been connected and acquainted with the value of city property and surrounding lands is the widely known house of Joseph Spence, located at room No. 1 Hancock Building, next to Postoffice. He has conducted this business for the past fourteen years and his long experience has made his services valuable in this line. He gives his careful attention to all interests of his patrons, which has won for him a large and lucrative business. Many of our most valuable property holders are numbered among his patrons, who have entrusted their business to his care for years. The buying, selling and exchanging of real estate, securing of loans, renting of property, paying of taxes, as may be desired, collecting of claims against the State, and general negotiations, come under the province of a real estate agent. In all these requirements Mr. Spence is not only familiar, but thoroughly reliable. His superior judgment and ability in the past is only an evidence of his future success. All his transactions are conducted upon a fair and honorable basis, giving to his patrons full satisfaction in every case.

B. C. WELLS—Jeweler; 614 Congress Avenue.

Located at No. 614 Congress Avenue in a desirable business portion of the city, is the jewelry establishment of B. C. Wells. This business was formed in 1871, and a successful trade has been the merited result of well directed effort. His sales room is ample and well fitted up and is stocked with a desirable and attractive line of imported and American watches from the most noted manufactories, together with clocks, solid silver and plated ware, jewelry of every description, fine cutlery, and articles for use and ornament, such as ordinarily pertain to first class metropolitan establishments of this description. His trade extends to all parts of the State supplying a large number of the country merchants with goods in addition to an extensive retail business. Mr. Wells is a practical and experienced jeweler, having thoroughly learned the trade, and this department is a prominent specialty of the business. He is a permanent resident of Austin, having lived here since 1871, and in conclusion we may state that he is liberal in his dealings, reliable and trustworthy, and he well merits the success and prosperity he has so long enjoyed.

E. M. PURKISS (Successor to Purkiss & Farr)—House, Sign and Ornamental Painter, Paper Hanger and Decorator; Wall Paper, Decorations and Painters' Supplies Wholesale and Retail; 919 Congress Avenue.

Among the most enterprising and substantial business houses of Austin is that of E. M. Purkiss, successor to Purkiss & Farr, which, established early in 1884, now ranks as the largest firm in its line in Austin or this section. He occupies the large and commodious building at 919 Congress Avenue, 22x80 feet, with a sign-room 40x50 feet in dimensions, both being handsomely fitted out with every convenience for the quick and systematic conduct of the business. He carries a large and complete stock of the best wall paper and decorations, with the largest line of paints in Austin. A force of twenty hands is employed whose work, both in house and sign painting and in paper

hanging and decorating, will bear comparison with any in the country.   Mr.
E. M. Purkiss possesses facilities which enable him to compete successfully
with all rivals.   Employing only experienced workmen, and he being perfectly familiar with both branches of the business, all work intrusted him
invariably gives satisfaction, and the numerous residences in Austin and the
State which have been fitted up by this house are evidences of his capacity to
guarantee satisfaction.   Mr. Purkiss is a gentleman well known in and out of
business circles, and with the present rapid growth of Austin, there is no
limit to his future extension.   All information concerning his business is cheerfully and promptly given, and estimates on work furnished on application to
him.

W. VON ROSENBERG—Land and General Agent; Office No. 826 Con-
gress Avenue, Corner West Ash Street.

Reviewing Austin in a business way we meet with many of the old and
substantial citizens who are worthy of mention in our history, and among
these is Mr. W. Von Rosenberg, general land agent.   He came to Austin as
early as 1856, and entered the Texas Land Office at once, which made him
quite familiar not only with the land, but with the land laws of the State, and
with the land business generally, and, therefore, is well qualified for the business he is conducting.   His advice and services are particularly valuable, as
they can be relied upon by land men as being correct.   Any parties wanting
taxes paid, land inspected and valued, purchased or sold, or any business
attended to in the several departments of the land offices, can commit their
interests to no abler or more prompt hands than to place them with Mr. Von
Rosenberg.   He is also a public spirited citizen enjoying offices of trust and
honor, the gifts of the people, and filling all such to the full satisfaction of the
public.   He is one of the directors of the new City National Bank.

RHOADS FISHER—(Formerly Chief Clerk General Land Office), Land
and General Agent; 816 Congress Avenue.

In the prepartion of the history of a city we often come in contact with
establishments and noteworthy enterprises that conduce so much to the public
welfare and which are in a measure unknown throughout the State.   Such we
desire in this volume to set before our readers.   In the general land business
in Austin we find Mr. Rhoads Fisher, who has been chief clerk in the General
Land Office, and therefore well fitted to offer his services to the public in this
line of business.   He is centrally located at 816 Congress Avenue, and makes
a specialty of purchasing and leasing of the school lands.   He pays taxes and
looks after lands generally, and devotes a portion of his time to the procuring
of patents, and understands the patent laws perfectly.   No one enjoys more

of the public confidence than Mr. Fisher, and none we are sure will conduct business entrusted to them with more marked ability or be more prompt in responding to their patrons than Mr. Fisher. We are glad to note the eminent success that is attending his untiring energy in this direction, and trust our readers who may have business in this line will feel assured of honorable and fair treatment at his hands for any trust that may be placed with him.

BARNES & SCOTT—WHOLESALE AND RETAIL DEALERS IN STAPLE AND FANCY GROCERIES; 101 AND 103 WEST PECAN STREET.

At the above named locality will be found one of the most elegantly fitted up and handsomely arranged family groceries in the city. The genial, popular, and enterprising gentlemen, Messrs. Barnes & Scott, will be found with the most complete, varied and carefully selected stock of staple and fancy groceries and general provisions to be found anywhere in the South, everything being new, fresh and clear. The building is large and admirably adapted to this business. The storerooms are light, commodious and neatly arranged with a tempting display of appetizing groceries of every conceivable kind; the best brands of flour, the choicest coffee, teas, sugar, syrups, spices, canned goods, hams, breakfast bacon, fruit and condiments of every kind, and in short, every article to be found in a first-class establishment of this description. The store is filled from one end to the other with as fresh and pure and as attractive a line of goods as can be desired or procured, and the stock is constantly kept up to the highest standard by frequent replenishments. This firm offer more advantages to the country community than most similar houses, as they deal in country produce of all kinds, and offer either cash or goods in payment for the same. They do the largest retail grocery business in Austin, and deliver goods free of charge to any part of the city, having two delivery wagons. Messrs. Barnes & Scott, the individual members of the firm, are well known in the city and surrounding country, and their energy, industry and integrity have secured them a position in the community entitling them to the respect and confidence as well as the liberal patronage of the public.

GRAHAM & ANDREWS—DRUGGISTS; 917 CONGRESS AVENUE.

Among the oldest and best established business houses of Austin is the one whose name heads our article, and which, throughout an existence of 30 years, has always preserved its high standing and reputation. Founded in 1854 by D. W. C. Baker, it became successively Baker & Graham, and in 1878 J. W. Graham; the present style being adopted a few months since by the admission of Mr. T. M. Andrews. The building is ample and commodious, being 40x120 feet in dimensions and two stories in height, and is well fitted out with every convenience for the prompt and successful conduct of the business. The stock consists of the very choicest and finest European and American drugs and chemicals, toilet articles, surgical instruments and other articles of a strictly first-class drug house. The prescription business which is their specialty, is as complete as any in Austin, their facilities for compounding being *the* best. A very large and complete line of paints and oils is also kept on hand, and is sold in direct competition with houses who deal exclusively in these articles. Messrs. J. W. Graham and T. M. Andrews, who comprise the firm, are both gentlemen of long and thorough experience in their business, and well known in trade circles and the social walks of life, as sterling business men and worthy citizens. It affords us pleasure to place among the representative firms of Austin, a house whose career has been so long and honorable as this one.

THOMSON & DONNAN—Land and Claim Agents, 808 Congress Avenue.

The conducting of the land and claim interest of Texas requires as much marked ability, sound judgment, keen foresight and promptness in action as any industry in the State. A volume designed to circulate largely over the State, information in this line of business, is more desirable than any other, as it tends to center business in Austin. Engaged in this branch of business is the firm of Thomson & Donnan, 808 Congress Avenue. Mr. R. M. Thomson and John K. Donnan compose the firm; both have been residents of Austin for years, and are familiar with the land interests of the State. They buy, sell and locate lands, pay taxes on the same, pay taxes for non-residents, and look after lands generally ; buy and sell land scrip, and handle land on commission, selling and making prompt returns. They are reliable men, as will appear plainly when we say they represent over 700 tracts of land, entrusted them by one man, who satisfied himself of their financial standing and upright business character by inquiry of different banks in the city, to whom they refer. As a firm with which to correspond and transact business, no better can be found, and none that exhibit more activity and carefulness, looking after the interests of their patrons with the same care and attention that they give their own.

L. SCHOOLHERR & BRO.—Dry Goods, 608 Congress Avenue.

One of the largest and most favorably known establishments in the dry goods line in Austin is that of L. Schoolherr & Bro., located at No. 608 Congress Avenue. This business was started about ten years ago, and has since the beginning been very successful. The building occupied for carrying on this business is located as above mentioned, and consists of two floors, 150x25 feet in dimensions, which are conveniently arranged for carrying on a business of this description. These gentlemen have constantly on hand a complete and choice stock of dry goods, notions, etc., at prices which will suit the most exacting purchaser. They are constantly replenishing their stock, thus keeping their goods fresh and of the latest styles and designs. About eight hands are employed as salesmen, and all patrons are treated in a very cordial manner. Besides having their share of the city trade, they receive considerable trade from the different sections of the State, and all orders receive prompt attention. Messrs. L. Schoolherr and S. Schoolherr are the individual members of the firm. They have had a life experience in this branch of business, and understand it in all its details. They have resided in the city for the last twelve years, are honorable, energetic business men, and well deserve the patronage of all our citizens.

PRESTON & SON—Architects; Rooms 5 and 6 (over Newman & Co.), 500 and 502 Congress Avenue.

Among the list of accomplished architects in this city, the house of Messrs. Preston & Son is a conspicuous one, especially for residences and public building work. Buildings after buildings have been erected during the past years from designs produced by these gentlemen, and they will stand for ages a monument of their master skill. Among the principal of these buildings are the North Texas Insane Asylum, State Deaf and Dumb Asylum, Court Houses for Bastrop, Washington, Bell, Cameron, Nolan, Taylor and Mitchell Counties, State Insane Asylum at Austin, J. L. Driskill's residence, Austin, and Jails for Cameron, Bell and San Saba Counties. They are also now preparing plans for the Driskill Hotel, of this city, costing $200,000. They are prepared to furnish designs and specifications, and superintend the erection of buildings of any character and description. Their trade is not confined alone to the city but extends throughout the State, and their services can be had by correspondents who live in any part of the State. They are courteous gentlemen in business transactions, liberal in their terms, and thoroughly experienced in their profession. Employment is given, when needed, to none but men of recognized ability, and they assure perfect satisfaction to all their patrons. Before closing we will say that they are high minded citizens of undoubted integrity in business and private affairs, and rank among the progressive men who delight to see Austin stand second to no city in the skilled arts and sciences which it fosters and encourages so extensively.

CALCASIEU LUMBER COMPANY—Yards at Austin and Elgin, Texas.

The lumber trade of Austin is a growing one and several good firms are engaged in it. The company heading this sketch is one of the best and in some respects possesses advantages not to be enjoyed by others. Some members of the firm are producers of the celebrated Calcasieu lumber from the Parish of that name in Louisiana; the grain and solidity and compactness of which makes the lumber far superior to the Texas pine, especially for dressing and inside work. They deal also in ash, cypress and hard wood lumber, doors, sashes, blinds, laths, shingles, pickets, posts, paints, oils, builders' hardware and everything necessary to build a house, and patent wire fencing of superior qualities as well, and at manufacturers' prices. The company was organized under the State laws of Texas two years ago. They have a river front as well as railroad facilities to carry on the business advantageously, and they deal as liberally with their patrons as any similar institution in the State. Mr. H. J. Sutchen is the president and Mr. W. S. Drake the secretary of the company, to which all communications regarding terms and prices should be addressed. We are glad to make space in our volume for this notice, as we belive our readers will be benefitted by learning of this firm and forming their business acquaintance. The marked successs attending this enterprise since starting is sure evidence that they compete successfully for the trade, and small dealers as well as builders of the surrounding country will have no cause to regret forming their acquaintance.

JOHN H. ROBINSON & SON—Wholesale and Retal Dealers in General Merchandise; 504 Congress Avenue.

In making a detailed review of the commercial interests of the city, prominent among these will be noticed the establishment of J. H. Robinson & Son which, from the special character of its business and the magnitude of its operations, should not escape mention in any work relating to the development, resources and industries of this city. This establishment was started thirty years ago by the senior member of the firm, but in 1869, Alf. H. Robinson, his son, was admitted as partner. They are located at No. 504 Congress Avenue, where they occupy two floors, 160x25 in size. They are retail dealers in general merchandise, as dry goods, groceries, boots, shoes, hats, caps, etc., and carry one of the largest and best assortments in the city. A specialty of this house is in furnishing outfits for stockmen when they start on the trail, and stockmen come from all parts of the surrounding country to get supplies of this kind. The advantages enjoyed by this firm in buying goods paying cash largely therefor, enables them to sell to the consumers at prices lower than most houses. These gentlemen have also invested largely in cattle, sheep and land, and we are glad to say, take a great interest in the State of Texas in every respect. Mr. J. H. Robinson, the senior member of this firm, and Mr. Alf. H., his son, are both gentlemen of large experience in this business, and all its operations are conducted under their personal supervision. To indulge in any personal laudation would be superfluous, and we need olny remark in conclusion, that the trade will find many advantages by establishing relations with this reliable house.

STUART FEMALE SEMINARY—1312 East Ash Street.

Austin is confessedly the educational centre of Texas, therefore, in reviewing her most prominent schools and colleges, a brief sketch of the above well-known institution is necessary. Stuart Seminary was founded in 1876, and

STUART FEMALE SEMINARY.

since its organization has had a well merited success, and now ranks among the best female educational institutions of the country. The building is admirably located on an elevation in the Eastern suburbs of the city, and commands a most magnificent view of the country for miles around. The long and varied experience of the Principal enable her to make its appointments with judgment, and her thorough knowledge of all its parts insures their proper use. Every precaution has been taken to secure the health of the pupils, both requiring moderate calisthenics, drill and furnishing balconies for promenade. The furniture is of the most improved pattern. There is also a chemical and philosophical apparatus. Stuart Seminary is one of the few institutions in which, to complete the course of studies, requires the utmost diligence and unremitting application. So rigid are the examinations, and so strict the requirements of graduation, that it probably numbers less full graduates on its roll than any Seminary in the country. Employing only the most competent teachers, and with a perfect system in all departments, Stuart Seminary may well challenge comparison. Mrs. R. K. Red, the principal, has had thirty years' experience in teaching, and has devoted her life to the building up of this institution, a feature in its history of which Austin may well be proud. It is the hope of all that this Seminary may long continue in its present course of honor and prosperity.

NEWMAN & CO.—Dealers in Dry and Fancy Goods, Corner Congress Avenue and Pine Street; Branch House, San Antonio, Tex.; New York Office, 97 Franklin Street.

Of the many handsome and spacious stores which line Congress Avenue, one of the best and most convenient in all respects is that of Messrs. Newman & Co., whose name heads our sketch. The building is 52x180 feet in dimensions and two stories in height, and is well lighted and ventilated, every convenience being provided for the rapid and systematic conduct of the business as well as the comfort of the numerous employees who number upwards of 40. The stock is the finest in Austin and probably in the State, comprising the finest dress goods and Parisian novelties, purchased in Europe by a member of of the firm who visits it every year for that purpose, thus placing their goods to their customers at first hands and avoiding middle men. The leading feature of Messrs. Newman & Co.'s establishment is, however, their dressmaking department, which, under the supervision of one of the most skillful lady dressmakers in America, enjoys a reputation far and wide for making dresses, cloaks, etc., which in design and finish are equal to any. As a proof of this we will mention that they have lately filled orders from Baltimore and Wyoming. Messrs. Samuel and Julius Newman and Philip Hatzfeld comprise the firm, all gentlemen well-known in and out of business circles, and numbered among the representative and enterprising citizens of Austin. They have also a large branch establishment at San Antonio, and their New York office is at

97 Franklin Street. It will then be seen that these gentlemen have connections and advantages possessed by no other firm in Austin, and having also ample capital they are enabled to offer their goods at manufacturers' prices. It affords us pleasure to write this sketch of one of the most substantial business houses in the South, and to advise our readers to visit their handsome establishment, in which they will see a display not surpassed by any similar firm in the country.

TILLOTSON COLLEGIATE AND NORMAL INSTITUTE. — East End Bois d'Arc Street.

Tillotson Collegiate and Normal Institute is one of the first objects which claim the attention of visitors to Austin. It is beautifully situated just east of the city, and commands a view of the valley of the Colorado, with its sur-roundings—rugged hills, fertile farms, shining waters, moving railroad trains, and last, but not least, the beautiful city of Austin—of which the eye never tires. This institution is devoted to the elevation of the Colored Race especially, though it knows no color—knowledge-seekers of all races are wel-come. It aims to produce human perfection. While the development of the intellect by a thorough mastery of the ordinary branches of knowledge is con-sidered of very great importance, the stimulation of the moral and religious nature holds a no less prominent place in the plan of the institution. A religious influence pervades the school, which makes itself felt for good on all who enter, and tends to secure application and consequent progress in all departments of the work. There are now in operation Intermediate, Gram-mar, Normal, College Preparatory, and Musical Departments, which are doing most thoroughly the work of corresponding departments in the best schools of the country. Other departments will probably be established when needed. There are accommodations for boarding eighty students. The authority and care exercised over the students of the boarding department is, as nearly as may be, like that of the Christian parent.

TERMS—PER MONTH.

Tuition, Intermediate and Grammar Departments............$2.00
Tuition, Normal and Preparatory Departments............... 2.50
Tuition, Instrumental Music Department................... 3.50
Board, including Tuition, Lights and Washing............12.00

Good board in private families can be procured at very reasonable rates. The school is open from October 1st to June 1st, with the exception of the last week in December. For further information, or catalogue, address,

TILLOTSON COLLEGIATE AND NORMAL INSTITUTE,
Austin, Texas.

A. K. HAWKES—Practical Optician, Inventor of Hawkes' Patent Extension Spring Eye-Glasses; Spectacles Adapted to all Conditions of the Eye.

Among the most attractive and handsomest of the many stores which line Congress Avenue is that of Mr. A. K. Hawkes, whose name heads our article. The building is 25x140 feet in dimensions, and two stories in height, and is fitted out with every convenience for the rapid and systematic conduct of the business. A complete stock of books, periodicals, stationery, and facny articles is carried, which are sold at most reasonable prices. Mr. Hawkes' specialty, however, is his renowned "Patent Extension Spring Eye-Glasses," which have attained a national reputation as the BEST Glass known, being adapted to all conditions of the eye. He imports his lenses direct from the most celebrated European makers and grinds them here; thus insuring as nearly perfect a lense as possible. These glasses are the result of many years research on the part of Mr. Hawkes, and they are undoubtedly one of the greatest boons to those who suffer in any degree from impaired sight. All communications are cheerfully and promptly answered. We append a few of the most prominent testimonials, of which Mr. Hawkes has a multitude from all parts of the Union.

One from the great revivalist, W. E. Penn:

Mr. A. K. Hawkes:

Dear Sir—I take great pleasure in saying that, after having worn your new crystalized lenses and patent spring eye-glasses for the past year, my sight has greatly improved. W. E. Penn.

New York City, April 7, 1884.

Mr. A. K Hawkes:

Dear Sir—Your patent eye-glasses and crystalized lenses, received some time since, and am very much gratified at the wonderful change that has come over my eye-sight since I have discarded my old glasses, and am now wearing yours. Alexander Agar,

Blank Book Manufacturer.

Mr. A. K. Hawkes:

Dear Sir—The spectacles you adapted to my sight nearly eight years ago, I am happy to say, enable me to see as clearly as the day I procured them, and I am now nearly eighty years of age. I cheerfully recommend them to the public. Respectfully, Wm. J. Russell,

Ex-District Judge.

HOUSTON, TEXAS, January 9, 1884.

MR. A. K. HAWKES:

Dear Sir—Since wearing your new crystalized lenses, my sight has greatly improved.   JOHN T. BRADY.

HOUSTON, TEXAS, March 12, 1884.

MR. A. K. HAWKES:

Dear Sir—I have now been wearing your glasses for nearly ten years, and I cannot see that my sight has failed in the least during this time.

Respectfully,   JAS. A. BAKER.

AUSTIN, TEXAS, March 3, 1881.

MR. A. K. HAWKES:

Dear Sir—I am much pleased with the pantiscopic glasses you so perfectly adapted to my eyes; with them I am enabled to read as in my youth, the finest print with greatest ease. I cheerfully recommend them to the public.

Respectfully,   R. B. HUBBARD,

Ex-Governor of Texas.

AUSTIN, TEXAS, August 7, 1881.

MR. A. K. HAWKES:

Dear Sir—The spectacles purchased from you nearly two years ago excel anything I have yet been able to procure. They enable me to read for hours with less fatigue to the eyes than any others that I have ever used.

E. B. TURNER,

Judge United State Court.

SPECIAL NOTICE.—The great reputation my spectacles have attained throughout Texas and the South, has led unscrupulous persons to counterfeit them. There are none genuine, unless the name of Hawkes is stamped on the bow. Send for catalogue and price-list.

A. K. HAWKES,

Austin, Texas.

MADDOX BROS. & ANDERSON—LAND AND REAL ESTATE AGENTS; 126 WEST PECAN STREET, NEAR POSTOFFICE.

The land and real estate interests of Austin are as prominent and important as any industry of the Capital City, and men of rare ability and vast capital are engaged in its transactions. Among the well known and competent firms we are called upon to mention, is the one heading this sketch. Their office is central, and as well fitted up to accommodate the business, and to accommodate the stockmen of the State, when in the city, as any similar establishment in the State, and is really headquarters for this class of men. The members of the firm are well informed business men, and conduct business in a straightforward business manner. They do a general real estate business. They buy and sell land certificates, examine and perfect titles, lands examined and divided, lands bought and sold, Patents obtained, taxes paid, lands redeemed, investments made, and give prompt attention to all business in General Land Office and other State departments. Our readers who may desire information upon any subject pertaining to land, real estate, ranche or stock enterprises, will find the firm prompt in answering, and capable of giving reliable information. They are actively connected with the Day Land and Cattle Company, having a paid-up capital of $510,000; one-third of which is owned by Maddox Bros. & Anderson. The success of the firm since starting in the real estate business a few years ago, is truly remarkable, and is the best recommendation any firm could possibly have of their executive ability, and we are sure that any business our readers may transact with them will prove a pleasant transaction, and be executed with marked ability and upright integrity.

C. A. DAHLICH—Manufacturer of and Dealer in Furniture and House Furnishing Goods, Carpets, Oil Cloths, etc.; Corner Colorado Street and North Avenue.

In our search for information regarding the furniture trade of this city, we were more than ordinarily attracted by the house of C. A. Dahlich, which was established by the present proprietor in 1874. He is located on the corner of Colorado street and North Avenue, and the salesroom is 60x100 feet in dimensions. He is manufacturer and dealer in furniture of every description, and also carries a well selected stock of carpets, oil cloths, etc. Being a manufacturer, he can sell at prices lower than most houses, as he has no expense in paying drayage and freight. Mr. C. A. Dahlich, the proprietor of this business, has had years of experience in this line, and understands it thoroughly in all its details. From its earliest establishment, this house has been a favorite source of supply in this line of trade, and those forming business relations with it will find a large and superior stock from which to make selection, as well as the pursuance of a liberal policy and an obliging promptness, such as is in accordance with an honorable record of so long standing.

EDWARDS & CO.—News Dealers and Stationers; 618 Congress Avenue.

The most extensive and elegantly appointed establishment in Austin in this branch of business is that conducted by Messrs. Edwards & Co., at No. 618 Congress Avenue. These gentlemen have been connected with this enterprise only two years, and the steady increase of trade since their commencement has been of a most gratifying character. This firm carry a full line of stationery and stationers' sundries, all the daily and weekly papers and magazines, chewing and smoking tobacco, fine cigars, etc.; are the sole agents for Foley's celebrated gold pens, and receive subscriptions for any periodical or magazine published. They receive a liberal order trade from all over the entire State, besides receiving the larger part of the city trade. Mr. Edwards has resided in this city since 1872 and is well-known both in social and commercial circles. He has had a number of years' experience in this trade, and thoroughly understands it in all its branches. In conclusion, we think it is quite within our province to commend this house to the trade, and to assure them that nothing will be left undone to make business relations between themselves and their customers permanent, pleasant and profitable.

W. A. GLASS—Wood and Coal Dealer; 113 West Cedar Street.

The coal industry of Austin is yearly becoming an enterprise of more magnitude, and as manufacturings increase, will grow still greater. The most prominent merchant perhaps in the trade is Mr. W. A. Glass, located at No. 113 West Cedar street, convenient to railroad facilities for handling coal, so that in price he can meet competition from any source. The quality of coal handled is of the very best grades for manufacturing or domestic purposes. He is prompt in supplying the people of Austin, and equally so in his attention given to orders received by mail. The continued prosperity of the house with an unsullied business record, is the best guarantee that it occupies a position of usefulness and confidence with the public generally, and is still worthy of their patronage. In wood, Mr. Glass can supply the entire city promptly and furnishes any length desired. He enjoys the best facilities to accommodate the public in this line, and deals in all kinds of hard and cedar wood, cedar posts and blocks. In connection with the coal and wood business he is also in the freight transfer line, moving iron safes, furniture and heavy goods generally; and all orders for this or the coal and wood departments remitted by mail, telephone or otherwise, receive the promptest attention.

J. H. COLLETT—Land and General Agent; 824 Congress Avenue.

The land interests generally in Austin are represented by men of ability and who have for many years made it a study. The agent heading this sketch is an old citizen and has been dealing in Texas lands since 1849. His business extends pretty much over the entire State, and he gives his attention to all the various departments of the land interests, and is fully competent to execute with ability any interests entrusted to him, either in way of perfecting titles, paying taxes, buying, selling, leasing, valuing land and looking after every interest in the land office. Our readers who desire interests promptly looked after, will find Mr. Collett will give them his attention and execute all matters with ability. He has the confidence of the public generally, and is a public spirited man, who rejoices at the prosperity of the city, and ready to aid in its public enterprises for its advancement to the front rank of the cities of the State.

ADOLPH BAHN — Watchmaker, Jeweler and Engraver; Congress Avenue.

There are few industries of the City of Austin which this comprehensive work will record, that require a higher order of skill or more refined taste in its operations, than that of the jewelry business; but the eminent success which has attended the establishment and conduct of this branch of trade by

Mr. Adolph Bahn is a sufficient evidence of his thorough adaptation to its requirements. This enterprise is the oldest of this kind in the city, it having been started as early as 1853. The salesroom occupied is 80x25 feet in size, and is kept constantly well stocked with a full assortment of clocks, watches, jewelry, spectacles, silverware, etc., all of standard makes and for sale at prices uniformly low and satisfactory. Repairing in all its departments is promptly attended to, and all work in this line is fully warranted. In addition, Mr. Bahn has an extensive manufacturing and diamond-setting department, and turns out some of the finest work to be had in this country, being equal to any of the eastern manufactories, with whom he can easily compete in price. Mr. Bahn is also the owner of a valuable patent of his own invention, being a combined napkin ring and holder, which certainly fills a long-felt want, combining the advantages of a napkin ring and a napkin holder, both to perfection. The accompanying cut will more fully explain its construction. Mr. Bahn invites special attention to this valuable patent, will be pleased to correspond with dealers in regard to the sale of rights for the sale of his patent. Mr. Bahn is a native of this city, and has been brought up in the jewelry business, learning the watchmaker's trade in Switzerland and the engraver's trade in New York. He is too well known to the trade to render necessary further personal mention, but, in conclusion, we will say that the success and facilities of this house, as well as the liberal and just business policy upon which it is conducted, have placed it above any of its cotemporaries and enables the proprietors to offer such advantages to the trade as will render business relations entered into with it permanent as well as profitable.

CHADWICK & DeCORDOVA—Insurance Agents; 704 Congress Avenue.

Regarding the importance and amount of insurance carried on in the City of Austin very few of our citizens have any accurate conception. Nevertheless some know it, and as a blessing to the widow and orphan; besides those who have suddenly been deprived of their houses by the ravages of the fire fiend, with the money secured by their insurance policy they are enabled to rebuild, and even in more modern style. Messrs. Chadwick and DeCordova are conducting at No. 704 Congress Avenue a general insurance business, upon honorable and upright business principles, fully understanding insurance in every detail. They have been in this business about four years, and represent most all the important companies on the face of the globe, some of which are given below: Ætna, Hartford; National, Hartford; Girard, Philadelphia; Fire Association, Philadelphia; Germania, New York; Citizens', New York; Hanover, New York; Crescent, New Orleans, La.; Lancashire, Eng.; Sun, of London; Commercial Union, London; Western, Toronto; Life Equitable, of New York; Accident Insurance Company of North America, and the entire assets of which are $125,000,000. The individual members of the firm are R. A. Chadwick, S. D. DeCordova and R. DeCordova, the latter two being members of the well-known firm of DeCordova & Son, land agents. These gentlemen are all too well known in commercial circles to require personal mention at our hands. As a firm, however, we may say that they combine a practical knowledge of the business, and long experience with unsurpassed facilities, which have added no little to the growth and prosperity of their house.

NALLE & CO—Dealers in Rough and Dressed Lumber of all Kinds, Sash, Doors, Blinds, Shingles, etc.; Yards and Office on East Avenue and Pine Street.

The lumber business, always of great importance to a city or community, is peculiarly so to one which is so rapidly increasing in population and business as this. Among the firms engaged in this important branch of commerce in Austin, Nalle & Co. are worthy of special mention, both by reason of the character and extent of the business done and because of the rare energy, activity and enterprise displayed in the management. Mr. Joseph Nalle, the sole member of the firm, the company being nominal only, is a native of Virginia, but has resided in Texas fourteen years. Thirteen years ago he established himself in the lumber trade, and from that time to the present has enjoyed a successful and prosperous career. At his yards on East Avenue and Pine street are kept all kinds of rough and dressed lumber, sash, doors, blinds, shingles, etc., for sale in any quantity and at the lowest prices. A mill situated at the yards dresses lumber of all kinds and cuts dimension stuff of any size, and enables Mr. Nalle to fill all orders at the shortest notice and in a most satisfactory manner. This is the largest lumber yard in the city, the stock carried being valued at $100,000, and purchasers will always find plenty of well-seasoned material from which to choose. Mr. Nalle also has lumber yards at Waco, Burnet and Alexander, and as he buys for all together, he enjoys great advantages in the way of low prices. This, together with the fact that the railroad track runs through his Austin yard, making the cost of shipping to and from it the very smallest, enables him to offer patrons inducements in the way of low prices, with which less favored rivals find it impossible to compete. The business of this establishment is conducted upon principles of the soundest commercial integrity and the broadest liberality, and carpenters, contractors, builders and others desiring to purchase lumber will find it to their advantage to call and learn the prices before purchasing elsewhere. We may be pardoned for mentioning here, as illustrative of Mr. Nalle's enterprise in business, that he is the owner of two cotton compresses, one at Waco and one at Ennis, each of which does a large business. Mr. Nalle is one of the public spirited citizens of Austin, a gentleman of genial manners and courteous address, and one with whom it is a pleasure to transact business.

WATERS-PIERCE OIL COMPANY—W. B. Abadie, Manager; Corner of Cypress and Nueces Streets.

The above company is a branch of the company of the same name whose headquarters are in St. Louis. The oils manufactured by this company are subjected to the severest tests before being put on the market, and consequently always give satisfaction. The lubricating oils are free from all the gummy properties which make other oils of inferior grade so objectionable, and the illuminating oil is perfectly safe under all circumstances. The company has a large warehouse here at the corner of Cypress and Nueces streets, and where are kept all the oils sold by them. Being situated convenient to railroad facilities here, they can handle oil economically, so that in price they can meet competition from any source. Oils for shipment to other points are loaded on the cars at the warehouse, thus avoiding all exposure to the sun and consequent leakage. Mr. W. B. Abadie, the manager of the Austin branch, is a gentleman of excellent standing, and to his executive ability is due, in a large measure, the present handsome and increasing business of this branch.

DeCORDOVA & SON—Texas Land and Tax Agency; 704 Congress Avenue.

In every city there are individual examples of men whose long connection in business pursuit and whose record for unflinching integrity and untiring industry make them objects of special note, not alone in their homes, but wherever commercial reputation is recognized and respected. There are few men in this city who have won for themselves and by their own exertion a higher rank among the land agents of Austin than Mr. DeCordova, the subject of this sketch. Coming here over thirty-five years ago he soon identified himself with land matters, and familiarized himself not only with the quality and value of lands, but with the land laws of the State, making his long experience, coupled with his superior judgment, of rare value to all who may be interested in land matters. He is senior member of the present firm of DeCordova & Son, land, tax and general agents for every county in Texas. If not the oldest, they are one of the oldest firms in the State. They deal in land warrants and certificates, and have lands for sale in nearly every county in the State. They pay taxes in every county in the State, examine lands, divide lands and prepare lands in such quantities as their patrons may desire, preparatory to selling the same. Titles are examined and perfected, and records made in the proper counties to which they belong. They invest money for capitalists and can do so where it will bring a good return by enhancement in value, either in trust deeds, vendors, liens, or land itself. They make prompt returns of all money received for sale of lands. To parties who have lands to sell or who wish to buy, or those who desire their land interests carefully looked after, we can commend them to no safer hands than theirs, and none certainly whose ability and reliability stands higher. Business relations, both pleasant and profitable, can be established by corresponding with the firm.

MRS. M. WILSON—Dealer in Millinery and Fancy Goods; 911 Congress Avenue.

The above well-known and popular establishment was commenced by Mrs. Wilson in 1877; and since its inception has enjoyed a large and rapidly increasing business which extends throughout the entire city and State and into Mexico. A force of experienced hands are employed, and the work done here has the reputation of being the best in Austin. A full stock of millinery is kept on hand and constantly replenished with the newest styles and fashions. The prices of this house are exceedingly moderate, and the work always gives satisfaction, hence results the popularity it enjoys. Parties here and elsewhere will find it to their advantage to call on or correspond with Mrs. Wilson. Orders are promptly filled, and any information cheerfully given.

ZIMPELMAN & BERGEN—Land and Insurance Agents; No. 105 East Pecan Street.

In compiling a work such as this, embracing a historical review of the business interests of the city, we take special pleasure in dwelling at some length upon those branches of business which are of the most general interest, and of giving somewhat more than a passing notice to the most prominent firms engaged in those branches. The business in which this city and State are most deeply interested at the present time is that of the real estate agent. All eyes have turned to Texas as offering the greatest inducements to capitalists wishing to invest their surplus funds in land, and thousands of dollars are annually pouring in here from the overflowing coffers of Northern and Eastern capitalists. It is of the first importance to a State, as well as to the parties immediately interested that the lands sold within her borders should be conveyed by titles that are beyond dispute, so that the least amount of litigation may arise therefrom, and that the State should be free from the odium consequent upon an unsettled and uncertain condition of land titles. Therefore the most credit for enterprise and progressiveness is not due to those real estate dealers who make the largest aggregate sales, but to those who give the best titles, and who do the most to settle the titles to all the lands, that the property of the State may be held by its proper owners and the courts less crowded with litigation growing out of conflicting claims to real estate. Among the firms in this city which have dealt largely in real estate, and whose transactions have been characterized by special attention to perfecting the titles of the lands sold, the firm of Zimpelman & Bergen occupies the first place. These gentlemen began business here in 1874, and recognizing the fact that honesty and reliablity are the foundation stones of a successful business career, they have endeavored to put themselves in such a position that when they recommend the title of a tract of land sold, it will prove to be as represented. So indefatigable have they been that they have now in their office a complete abstract of the title to every city lot or out lot in the city of Austin, and of every tract of land in the county of Travis. This is the only firm in the city in possession of a complete abstract of these titles, and they are, therefore, in better position to look after the interests of non-resident owners, and to buy and sell real estate in the city and county than any other firm in existence. They have, also, a copy of all the early records of Travis Land District, affecting the titles to lands in the counties of Hays, Comal, Blanco, Burnet, Llano, Lampasas, San Saba, Brown, Coleman, Runnels, Callahan, Taylor, and others. Besides this they have access to the records of the General Land Office, and are fully prepared to give information concerning lands in any part of the State. They do a general land business, buying and selling city property, farms, ranches and timber lands, of which they have a variety on hand at all times. They act as agents for non-resident land owners, paying taxes, collecting rents, and transacting all other business in the most satisfactory manner. They also negotiate loans for parties desiring to borrow money on real security, and as they represent persons and corporations controlling large capital, money can be procured through them at the lowest rates of interest. This firm also do a general fire insurance business, being resident agents of the North British Mercantile, Hamburg-Bremen, Phœnix, of London and New Orleans, all of which are among the most solid and substantial fire companies of the world. The *personnel* of this firm is composed of Messrs. George B. Zimpelman, James V. Bergen, J. H. Daniel, and C. W. Daniel, all gentlemen who are well-known in business circles for the enterprise and progressiveness, as well as the honesty and integrity which characterize their transactions. The Messrs. Daniel attend to the general business of the firm, the time of the other members being largely engrossed by their private affairs. The transactions of this house are all conducted upon principles of the broadest and most advanced liberality, and the members of the firm, individually and collectively, are regarded as among the most enterprising and public spirited business men of the city. We cordially recommend this firm to our readers as one upon whose representations they may rely implicitly, and one with which dealings will always be found both pleasant and profitable. A list of prices will be furnished upon application, and persons desiring to invest money in lands, in any part of the State, will find it to be to their advantage to correspond with Messrs. Zimpelman & Bergen, No. 105 East Pecan Street.

GETTINS, BOBO & CO.—Land, Loan and Collections; No. 914 Congress Avenue.

Of late years the attention of the overcrowded parts, North, East and in Europe, have been attracted to the fertile soil of Texas, and as its resources and inducements are now well-known, immigration has set towards this State. Of all the States in the Union, Texas is the largest and richest, and has well estab-

lished the fact that for soil and climate is unsurpassed anywhere. The firm heading this notice is a very valuable acquisition to Austin, as their extensive connection with Europe tends to bring to our city capitalists who are seeking investment for money. They offer their services in making large loans to parties who may desire loans on lands or ranches, and for such term of years as may be desired. They are able, also, to place large tracts of land in the East and Europe at advantageous rates to purchasers. Their knowledge of the topography of Texas and its resources, enable them to place money for capitalists in lands that are sure to bring a good return by the rapid enhancement in value, or on loans at liberal interest. They have a large correspondence with Mexico, England, Scotland and Germany, and besides dealing in lands, mining property receives a share of their attention, and good mines can be sold or stocked by them in England and Scotland, through a syndicate of capitalists they work with under a special agreement. This business is conducted upon a broad basis of liberality and fair dealings, and they are prompt in their correspondence and faithful to their patrons' interests. A specialty of the house is in representing an English patent for meat slaughtering and preserving. The firm is ready to negotiate with stockmen, who desire to slaughter their fat beeves for shipment to Europe or the Eastern States. They have secured from the patentee in England, the right to grant licenses to such companies. By this process the meat can be shipped to any part of the world without refrigerators or ice, and be in perfect condition so long as it is kept below 55 degrees of zero. Readers may rest assured of receiving at the hands of this firm pleasant and profitable business relations.

MISS MARY E. FRANKS—Dressmaker; Congress Avenue, Corner Bois d'Arc Street.

Miss Franks is a lady well-known in Austin, where she has resided sixteen years, always enjoying a liberal share of the most desirable patronage in the city and State. Her work invariably gives satisfaction in all respects, and orders from any point receive prompt attention. Any information regarding her business is cheerfully given, and parties here and elsewhere will find it to their advantage to call on or correspond with her in matters pertaining to her business.

JOHN A. WEBB & BRO.—Agricultural Implements and Wagons; 212, 214 and 216 East Pecan Street.

Texas is rapidly becoming the greatest farming region of America or the world; hence those firms which deal in farming implements, wagons, etc., have a peculiar claim on the attention of our people. In this connection we give a sketch of the house of John A. Webb & Bro. This firm was founded in 1871, and from its inception took a leading position. They occupy the immense building numbered 212, 214 and 216 East Pecan Street, 79x128 feet in dimensions, and two stories in height. The building is substantially constructed, and provided with every convenience for the rapid and systematic conduct of their business. Their trade, which reaches a large and fast increasing annual sum total, extends throughout the city and adjoining counties. Messrs. J. A. Webb & Bro. carry a complete line, being agents for the celebrated Cooper, Whitewater and Studebaker wagons; the world-renowned Glidden barb wire, made by the Washburn & Moen Manufacturing Co., of Worcester, Mass., the largest manufacturers of barb wire in the world, and the well-known Malta cultivators and double shovels. They are also agents for the Moline Plow Co.'s goods, made at Moline, Illinois. They also carry an assortment of farm implements, wagons, buggies, threshers, mowers, reapers, engines, plows, gins and rubber belting, which, being bought direct from the factories, are placed to the trade at bottom prices. Messrs. John A. Webb and Joseph W.

Webb, who compose the firm, are gentlemen of the highest standing in business circles, and worthy members of society. Possessing ample experience and fine facilities, they can invite competition from any source, and parties here and elsewhere will find it to their interest to correspond with or call on them. All communications are promptly answered and information in all points regarding their business given. With the present rapid growth of Austin, their business has no limit to its future extension.

THE NEW AND PURITY TEA AND COFFEE STORE—J. C. BEALL, PROPRIETOR; 910 CONGRESS AVENUE.

This new enterprise has but recently been started, but from appearances it proves to be one of the most important of this kind in the city. Mr. J. C. Beall, the sole proprietor, has been a resident of Austin since 1881, and he ranks high both in business and social circles. He is very favorably located at No. 910 Congress Avenue, and his store is arranged in a neat and attractive manner. He carries a full line of all teas and coffees, namely: Old Government Java, Santos, Mocha, Laguayra, etc., pure spices, sugars, molasses, flour, rice, pickles, sauces, milk, preserves, jellies, etc., all guaranteed to be fresh and pure, and at the very lowest prices. Orders are solicited for everything in the grocery line, and goods are delivered to any part of the city free of charge. From facts at hand, we feel justified in saying that all who effect relations with this house will derive advantages that cannot readily be accorded elsewhere.

THE ERIE TELEGRAPH AND TELEPHONE COMPANY—J. K. DUNBAR, GENERAL SUPERINTENDENT.

One of the most important enterprises connected with the prosperity and growth of Austin is the Erie Telegraph and Telephone Company, whose headquarters for Texas and Arkansas are situated here. Established in Austin in 1881, its growth has been exceedingly rapid, and it now numbers on its list the principal firms of Texas, as well as many private houses. A total of fifteen persons are employed in Austin, seven in the general office and eight in the exchange office, and upwards of 500 are employed in Texas and Arkansas. There is connection with the following towns: New Braunfels, Baird, Bertram, Burnet, Boerne, Belton, Comanche, Coleman, Fredericksburg, Georgetown, Lampasas, Leon Springs, Lockhart, Round Rock, Eagle Pass, Temple, Salado, and many others. There will soon be connection between Temple and Waco, which will add 125 towns to the list, thus vastly increasing its already great facilities. The Company use the best and most improved telephones only, and its corps of officers and assistants is efficient and active. The officers are: J. K. Dunbar, Superintendent; J. O. Carruthers, Auditor; W. H. Pillow, Superintendent of Supplies, in Austin; and W. A. Ingam, President, and Chas. J. Glidden,

Treasurer, Lowell, Massachusetts; J. P. McKinistry, General Superintendent, Cleveland, Ohio. Being on a substantial basis, pecuniary and otherwise, the future of this company is as well assured as that of any corporation in the country, and will long continue to form, as it does now, a very integral part of the business interest of Austin. With the universal use of the telephone throughout the Union, no house who would keep up with the times can afford to be without one of this company's instruments in its office.

T. P. ROBINSON—Hides and Wool; 608 and 610 East Pecan Street.

In reviewing the business interests of Austin, the enterprise whose name heads our article is deserving an important place. Mr. Robinson established his business in 1880, and since that time, has increased it in a very gratifying extent indeed. He enjoys facilities possessed by no other similar firm in Austin. Mr. Robinson is enabled to give the very highest cash prices for wool and hides, and parties who have these articles on sale will do well to call or correspond with him. Mr. Robinson is a gentleman well known and esteemed, and with the rapid growth of Austin and the State, there are no limits to the future extension of his business.

UNDERHILL & CO.—Proprietors Austin Marble Works, Manufacturers and Dealers in Native and Imported Marble and Granite; Northwest Corner Capitol Square.

Of the many industries that employ a higher grade of skilled labor, and one rising above the mere power of mechanical skill and verging into the artistic, is that of the marble and monumental works of the country. Within the past few years the cemeteries of our cities have become attractive spots for visitors, on account of their many beautiful monuments and headstones. There is no establishment in Austin that has contributed more in this respect than the one whose name heads this sketch. Messrs. R. B. Underhill and A. J. Jernigan are the individual members of the firm, which was established in the business here in 1880. Their buildings and yards are located on the northwest corner of the Capitol Square, and embrace about three-fourths of an acre, for the successful production of all the finer grades of work pertaining to the art, and employment is given to as many as twelve or fifteen skilled artisans in the busy season. They manufacture tombstones, monuments, statues, statuettes, busts, medallions, plaster casts, mantels, grates, terra cotta work, vases, lawn chairs and iron fencing, and also do modeling and designing. For quality of stock and artistic skill in finish, the work turned out here cannot be surpassed by any other establishment. The trade not only receives a local demand, but demands from all parts of the State, and to some extent from Mexico, which may be regarded as a just tribute to energy and superior workmanship. The proprietors give their personal supervision to all the details of their popular establishment, thus ensuring to patrons and customers the most perfect and complete satisfaction. This enterprise is well worthy the attention of our many readers throughout the South, and as an important addition to the industries of Austin is entitled to the special recognition which it has been accorded in the present volume.

W. MOSES & SON—MERCHANT TAILORS, DEALERS IN FINE CLOTHING, GENTS' FURNISHING GOODS, HATS, TRUNKS, VALISES, ETC.; 613 CONGRESS AVENUE.

Undoubtedly the leading establishment in Austin in the clothing and gents' furnishing goods line is that of Messrs. Moses & Son, which, located in the most fashionable portion of the city, has for some time occupied without dispute this position. This firm carry a very large and select stock of goods, embracing fine clothing, gents' furnishing goods, hats, trunks, valises, and, in short, every article found in a first-class establishment of this description. These gentlemen are also merchant tailors, and among their many regular customers will be found many of the most prominent citizens and business men of the State. Thoroughly acquainted with the grades of the Northern markets, they are always enabled to purchase the best of everything, selecting their goods with the skill of those long accustomed to this business. Their present position as leaders of the fashion of Austin, has been obtained by unceasing application to business, and a nice appreciation of the wants of their customers, and we can safely recommend them to all who wish the best goods in Austin at the most reasonable prices.

JOHN BREMOND—WOLESALE DEALER IN DRY GOODS, BOOTS, SHOES, HATS FURNISHING GOODS, GROCERIES, ETC.; 109, 111 AND 113 EAST PECAN STREET.

Among the names of those who have been foremost in adding to the commercial importance of Austin, and in extending her trade, there is none more conspicuous than that of John Bremond. John Bremond, the elder, came here from Philadelphia, and established a general mercantile and banking business thirty-nine years ago, and though the business long ago passed from its founder to his two sons, and was divided between them, the head of the mercantile house is still John Bremond, and that name is to-day, as it has been for years, of the first importance in Austin's commercial calender. The building occupied by Mr. Bremond is a two story brick structure, 70x165 feet in area, with a one story warehouse attached, covering a space of 80x128 feet, each building having a dry cellar. These two buildings afford an immense amount of room, but no more than is required for the accommodation of the stock carried. This stock embraces a full and complete line of dry goods, boots, shoes, hats, notions, furnishing goods, and groceries, including the best and most popular brands known to the market, all bought with special reference to the trade for which they were intended, and selected with that careful and discriminating judgment which can only be acquired by great practical experience. This house, having a larger trade than any similar institution in the city, buys its goods for cash in greater quantities, thus being able to procure them at the lowest possible prices. This, together with the unrivaled facilities which it has for handling its stock at small cost, enables it to offer customers inducements in the way of low prices, which less favored competitors find it impossible to duplicate. Mr. Bremond, conducts his business upon the most conservative methods, paying careful attention to the *quality* of his trade, rather than to its *quantity*, the long established, unimpeachable reputation of his house bringing to him the most desirable patronage of the surrounding country, and enabling him to be independent of those customers whose trade is accompanied by more than a minimum risk. His patrons are his friends, and it is a fact which partakes of the phenomenal, and one in which he is justified in feeling a pride, that of the millions of dollars which his trade has aggregated during the last seventeen years, his losses have been *very* small. For a retail house to be able to open an account with the house of John Bremond, is a compliment to its commercial standing, and the honesty and, integrity of its management. It is such houses as this that have added most to the honor and dignity of the commercial world, and which do the most for the development, growth and prosperity of a city.

PADGITT & WARMOTH—Manufacturers of Saddlery, and Wholesale Dealers in Saddlery Hardware, Leather, Boot and Shoe Findings, etc.; 304 and 306 East Pecan Street. Branch Houses, Dallas, Waco, Fort Worth, Bryan, Mexia and Brownwood.

In reviewing the large and increasing business interests of Austin, the manufacturing and wholesale houses naturally take the first place ; hence a detailed sketch of the firm of Padgitt & Warmoth, who rank among the largest manufacturers in their line, not only in Texas, but the South, is necessary. Established in 1877, from their inception they took a leading position, and to-day they carry an immense stock, aggregating $60,000 in value, while their sales, which extend throughout Texas, Arkansas, Louisiana, Tennessee and Mississippi, reach nearly half a million dollars annually, and are rapidly increasing. This splendid result is due to superior quality of goods manufactured by this firm, their goods for quality, finish, durability and cheapness competing favorably with those of Northern and Western houses. Their store, which is one of the finest for business purposes in Texas, is 36x120 feet in dimensions, and two stories in height; is thoroughly fitted out and admirably lighted and ventilated. Upwards of twenty skilled hands are employed, who manufacture all styles of saddlery, horses' and mules' outfits, straps, etc., and a large stock of fine leather and boot and shoe findings is also kept on hand for the trade. The firm make a specialty of saddle girths, which, manufactured from their own designs, have a wide and favorable reputation. Messrs. Tom Padgitt and G. H. Warmoth compose the firm; Mr. Warmoth being the resident partner and conducting the business. Both gentlemen are well known in and out of business circles, and have had long and thorough experience in their business. Possessing ample capital and facilities, they offer inducements to buyers which few can duplicate, and parties here and elsewhere will find it to their advantage to call on them or correspond with them. All communications are promptly answered, and a comparison of prices invited. They will also furnish on application a fine illustrated catalogue of 77 pages, from which any information can be obtained.

MRS. M. A. McCLURE—Dealer in Staple and Fancy Groceries, Produce, Fruits, Tobacco, Cigars, etc.; 906 Congress Avenue.

In the compiling of a work of this character, every business venture that evidences genuine enterprise and energy is entitled to due consideration in its pages. A well located, well arranged grocery is of special interest to the housekeepers, inspiring them as it does with confidence that they will be furnished with choice, fresh articles for family consumption. The establishment of Mrs. M. A. McClure is pre-eminently one of this class. She deals in all kinds of staple and fancy groceries, produce, fruits, tobacco, cigars, and, in fact, all articles found in a first-class grocery. Her trade is mostly confined to the city, and goods are delivered to any part of the city free of charge. Her two sons assist her in carrying on this enterprise and prompt attention is given to the wants of all patrons. Mrs. McClure has conducted this business for the last twelve years; she is well-known and highly esteemed in business circles, and enjoys an enviable reputation as a straight-forward, honorable dealer, and to this fact is due the flourishing trade she has built up.

MADAME E. F. DUKE—Proprietor of "Templeton's Eye Water" and "Dr. Harland's Medicated Baths;" 118 East Bois d'Arc Street.

Among the modern inventions of science which have conferred the greatest benefits on mankind, we must mention the above renowned remedies. Madame Duke has introduced these remedies in spite of all the opposition of envious physicians, whose patients, almost blinded by *their* mode of treatment, came to this lady and were cured. Hundreds of testimonials from all parts of the country testify to the marvelous efficacy of "Templeton's Eye Water," and many in Austin and the surrounding country to-day see and read without difficulty, who, when first placed under her treatment, were nearly blinded. Her "Dr. Harland's Medicated Baths" are also the best known cure for rheumatism, neuralgia, sciatica, blood poisoning, and all diseases of that class. Some of the most prominent ladies and gentlemen (among them a well known *physician*) of Austin, and other places have been thoroughly cured by these baths. Madame Duke cheerfully gives any information regarding her remedies; and orders for the Eye Water receive prompt attention, as it is shipped by express to any part of the United States. She has ample accommodations for patients who desire a course of treatment; and those afflicted either with sore eyes, rheumatism, blood poisoning, sciatica, etc., will find it a lasting advantage to call on or correspond with her.

READ WHAT THE PEOPLE SAY ABOUT THE EYE WATER:

OLD ROUND ROCK, Williamson County.

I do certify that I went blind in 1863, from working for the Confederate Government making salt, and then for my blindness I tried everything I ever heard of, but all failed. In 1872, I went entirely blind and remained so until 1876, when my eyes became raw from extreme inflammation that the lids were growing together; then I got so that I could get about. The nerves being so badly injured that I was in a blind. I then commenced using eye water known as Templeton's Eye Water, and my eye-sight is sufficiently good for me to read and write for a short time. I believe it to be the best Eye Water now in use for all chronic cases of sore eyes. It is a sure remedy if used according to directions, and for which, gentlemen, I am under many obligations to you for this great remedy that has restored my sight again. So I return many thanks to you and my God.

February 15, 1882. S. J. HICKS.

OLD ROUND ROCK, February 15, 1882.

This is to certify that I have used the Templeton Eye Water with great success. On one occasion my wife got a scale of concentrated lye in her eye, and she suffered great pain for five days; upon an application of Templeton's Eye Water she got instant relief. I know an old lady who was blind from a cataract on her eyes and was cured by using Templeton's Eye Water. I could mention many others who have been cured, but a word to the wise is sufficient.

Yours truly, JAS. G. HARRELL.

ROUND ROCK, February 14, 1882.

This is to certify that my brother-in-law's family (nine in number), were all taken with inflammatory sore eyes. Their eyes were so much swollen and as red as blood, so that they could not bear the light of day upon them. I advised them to use Templeton's Eye Water. They got two bottles, costing fifty cents, and it cured them all sound in five days. My advice to all persons afflicted with chronic or inflammatory sore eyes is to use Templeton's Eye Water, as I know hundreds of cases in our midst that it has cured.

D. M. Kent, Marshal of Round Rock.

Dr. Templeton:—In behalf of the suffering and blind, I want to thank God and you for the great discovery of your excellent Eye Water. I resided and practiced medicine in connection with Dr. Ideld, in France, who was a celebrated oculist. But in many cases he failed to effect a cure, but your Eye Water, in every instance, has proved a success. One gentleman came to me for treatment, whose eyes I examined and found so granulated, that I saw no chance for a cure and refused treatment. However, I gave him the samples you left with me and they cured him sound and well. My brother-in-law had chronic sore eyes and finally went entirely blind. He tried many of the best oculists in New Orleans and Mobile, but found no relief. Upon my recommendation he tried your Eye Water, and was soon able to read a newspaper. I have used it in my practice and can heartily recommend it to all who are afflicted with sore eyes. I would to God that it could reach the world of suffering and blind. Please send me another supply.

Your grateful friend, B. T. Crumly, M. D.

Austin, January 8, 1883.

This is to certify that I was cured of neuralgia by Mrs. E. F. Duke, which has not returned since. I consider myself permanently cured. Miss Jennie Haux, Mrs. F. C. McKinney, Mrs. M. L. Nixon, Mrs. Nan. E. Ooley, and Mrs. Mary Coats. Office in Brown's Red Brick.

STEWART & HABICHT—Law, Claim, Banking and Collection Office; 716 Congress Avenue.

In the standing and responsibility of its business houses, Austin need not fear comparison with any city in the country. Hence, in reviewing the most prominent firms, a detailed notice of the well-known one whose name heads our article is necessary. The firm of Stewart & Habicht transact a law, claim, banking and general collection business in all its branches; render and pay taxes for non-residents, and perfect titles to lands; also buying and selling lands on commission. They have peculiarly favorable facilities for tracing out and perfecting weak or imperfect titles. Their correspondents are found all over the Union, and this, combined with their long and varied experience, render them thoroughly fitted to successfully transact their business in all its details. Messrs. Joe H. Stewart and A. E. Habicht, who compose the firm, are both gentlemen well known in and out of business circles. Parties here and elsewhere having business in their line will find it to their advantage to call on or correspond with them, as all dealings are invariably satisfactory, promptness and thoroughness being their rules.

R. T. BANDY—(Successor to Bandy & Parker), Saddlery and Harness; 209 East Pecan Street.

Among the most progressive and enterprising houses of Austin, we must mention the one whose name heads our list; and which, established in 1878, from its inception took a leading position. Mr. Bandy occupies a building 24x120 feet in dimensions, well fitted out and equipped with every conven-

ience for the prompt and systematic conduct of the business. He employs a large and skillful force of workmen, and his trade, which reaches a large and constantly increasing amount, extends throughout the city, State, Colorado, Kansas, Nebraska, New Mexico, Arkansas and Louisiana. The work done here will compare favorably with any in the country; and prompt attention is given to all orders. While manufacturing all lines of saddlery and harness, Mr. Bandy makes a specialty of cowmen's outfits, stock saddles and light harness, for which he has a reputation unequaled in Austin. Mr. Bandy is a gentleman well known in and out of business circles, and parties here and elsewhere will find it to their advantage to call on or correspond with him.

CARROLLTON HOUSE—West Pecan Street, Half Block West of the Postoffice; Dr. A. D. Harn, Proprietor.

Among the public houses in this city there are none enjoying a higher reputation for the embodiment of every requisite essential in a first-class hotel than that of the well-known Carrollton House, on West Pecan street. In the first place, the location of this hotel is the most eligible, being situated near the business center of the city, convenient to almost any point, and but half a square from the postoffice. In the second place, the building in all its appointments and equipments, is admirably adapted to the purpose for which it is used; and in the third place, its proprietor and attaches are experienced and efficient in their duties as caterers to the public, making the Carrollton House particularly inviting to the traveling community desiring practical conveniencies and comforts. This house is a two-story frame building, with pleasant, well ventilated apartments, sufficient to accommodate fifty to seventy-five guests; a large and conveniently appointed office, handsomely furnished reception rooms, ample baggage rooms, and a dining room especially inviting in every feature requisite to establish a feeling of comfort, peace and good will among guests, while satisfying the inner wants of nature. In every respect, the "Carrollton" is a first-class hotel, not surpassed by any in the city, and under the able management of Dr. A. D. Harn, holds a high rank among Austin's famous institutions for public entertainment. Mr. Harn has been conducting this business for the past eight years, and understands it thoroughly in all its branches. He has an extensive acquaintance with the traveling public, and his personal popularity will always insure the Carrollton House a generous support.

AUSTIN COAL CO.—MATTINGSLEY & CO., AGENTS; CORNER OF COLORADO AND RAILROAD TRACK.

Situated most conveniently to the railroad is the office and sheds of this extensive coal company, thus avoiding all unnecessary expense in handling this heavy article of commerce. They have provided every facility to conduct this business in an economical manner, and their patrons may rest assured they are as well cared for as any in the State. They handle all kinds of bituminous and anthracite coal, and make a specialty of the celebrated Indian Territory coal that has become so famous in Texas. They deliver coal to all parts of the city with despatch, and no orders are neglected. Merchants and dealers along the line of the railroad will find as fair and honorable dealings at the hands of this enterprising firm as they could ask or have a right to expect. We can cheerfully commend our readers, who do business in this line, to this wholesale and retail coal company, and can assure them that they will receive at their hands as many decided advantages as can be found in the State of Texas.

C. R. JOHNS & SONS—TEXAS STATE AGENCY; 1000 CONGRESS AVENUE.

Texas, with her millions of acres of land, will always need men of experience and sound judgment to represent these among settlers, speculators and land dealers generally. Among the oldest and ablest conducted enterprises in this line is the Texas State Agency, incorporated under the State laws of Texas in June, 1884. This company is an outgrowth of an enterprise of this character started by Mr. C. R. Johns, the President of the present company, many years ago, and for which he was well fitted by being previously connected with the public offices, and was comptroller for several years. He was born near Murfreesborough, Tennessee, and came to Texas in an early day, about 1836, and has filled many offices of trust and honor. His two sons, Tom D. and J. P. Johns, were born in Texas, reared practically to the business, and now, in the prime of life, are giving their entire energy to the business. Mr. H. L. Haynes manages the tax department, and Mr. S. G. Sneed has charge of the chief land department. They conduct a general land business over the entire State, own large tracts of land which have been acquired at bargains and can be sold at remarkably low figures, and do a general land business on commission. They attend to the assessment and payment of taxes in Counties and Comptroller's office; inspection of lands and report as to quality, value and occupancy; adjustment of titles and recovery of interest in lands; business of every character in General Land Office; purchase, sale, lease and protection of lands; redemption of lands sold for taxes; investment and loan of money; collection of claims against the State and settlement of collectors' and other accounts; business with the several departments of the State government. They have within secured walls first-class fire proof vaults where valuable papers of all kinds, such as bonds, deeds, mortgages, title papers of all kinds can be safely cared for. With these facilities and the long experience in this business which they have had, makes the firm one of the most desirable to form the acquaintance of, and consult on any matters connected with the land business, and any business conducted at this office will prove entirely satisfactory, and lands passing through their hands will be found, as regards title, perfect in every particular. We can safely say to our readers, who desire any information on lands, that they will consult their own interests when they correspond and form the acquaintance of this truly reliable company. It is impossible in an article of this character, to set forth all the details of their business, and we can only advise our patrons to correspond with them for particulars, and they will be found prompt and pleasant correspondents.

NEWNING, TURNER & WARNER—REAL ESTATE AND INSURANCE AGENTS; 720 CONGRESS AVENUE.

This company is composed of experienced real estate and insurance agents, well known to the people of Austin and the State of Texas. The individual members of the firm are Messrs. Chas. A. Newning, Fred W. Turner and Geo. P. Warner, all enterprising men and in the prime of life. They conduct a general real estate business in all its branches, embracing abstracting, loaning, paying taxes, looking after estates generally, both in and out of the city, and all business with the State Department. This firm have for sale large and small bodies of land in the counties adjoining Travis county, composed of the richest black soil for farming purposes, land that will raise a bale of cotton per acre, and cerial crops in proportion. Much of this land is already in cultivation, and new comers can yet be supplied with unbroken lands at low figures. They will gladly correspond with parties desirous of further details and descriptions. Besides the local real estate business they give special attention to the buying and selling of ranches and stock of all kinds. Their insurance department is ably conducted in the interest of the following companies: Phœnix, of Brooklyn; American, Philadelphia; Niagara, New York; Fireman's Fund, San Francisco; Western, San Francisco; Sun, San Francisco; Trans-Atlantic, Hamburg, Germany; British America, Toronto; Union F. & M., New Zealand; St. Paul, St. Paul. Each member of the firm has held responsible positions in the community where they reside. Mr. Turner is the special State agent and adjuster for the British America Assurance Co. of Toronto, Canada. Mr. Warner is Secretary of the Austin Savings and Loan Association. The firm respectfully refer to any banker in the city.

CRYSTAL SALOON—Charles Cortissoz, Proprietor; Corner Congress Avenue and Pecan Street.

Austin, among her other attractions, may boast of possessing the finest saloon and billiard parlor not only in Texas, but south of New York. We refer to the well-known "Crystal" Saloon, of which Mr. Charles Cortissoz is the genial proprietor. The "Crystal" is fitted out in the most elegant and tasteful manner, with every convenience and luxury, regardless of cost. The finest and costliest woods, cherry and mahogany only, are used; the interior doors leading from the bar to the billiard parlor are of ground glass of the most expensive quality, and the other equipments, decanters, glasses, etc., are on an equally fine scale. The billiard parlor is decorated with the costliest wall papers, paintings, etc., and three fine billiard tables and one pool table complete the sum of its attractions. The liquors sold by the "Crystal" are the best to be found in Austin; and, in fact, we have no hesitation in pronouncing this saloon the equal of any in the country. We cordially recommend it to all who visit Austin as well worthy a visit; and we may add that all are welcomed by Mr. Cortissoz, who takes a natural pride in his beautiful place.

A. M. C. NIXON—Architect; 623 Congress Avenue.

The profession of the architect is in all places one of the most important, and especially so in Texas, which is growing so rapidly and with such vigor. Austin, as the capital of the State, may boast of possessing some of the finest public buildings, and private dwellings in this section; hence, in reviewing the many industries and professions which compose the sum of her business interests, it behooves us to mention the architect who has planned the structures at once substantial and elegant. Mr. A. M. C. Nixon, whose name heads our article, since establishing himself at Austin, has gained a wide reputation as a capable and talented architect, and has built up a business which enables him to limit himself to one line of his profession, namely, churches, opera houses, and private buildings. Among his best known works are: the Georgetown

Methodist Church, and the Episcopal Church; remodeled entirely, German
Lutheran Church, Methodist Church, two Colored Churches, in this city. He has
also remodeled the Market House of Austin. Besides these, numerous splendid private buildings throughout the State and city attest his skill. Mr. Nixon
is a gentleman well known in and out of business circles, and has had a long
and thorough training at his profession, serving his time and pursuing his studies
with one of the most celebrated English architects, Alfred Derbyshire, Esq., F.
R. I. B. A. We cheerfully recommend Mr. Nixon to all interested in the erection of private buildings and other edifices, and they will do well to call on or
correspond with him.

F. SCHMITZ—Dealer in Furniture and Carpets, Manufacturer of Mat-
      tresses and Spring Bottoms; 205 East Pecan Street.

Among the best known and most enterprising establishments of Austin, is
that of Mr. F. Schmitz, whose name heads our article. He occupies the commodious building, No. 205 East Pecan Street, which is well fitted out with every
convenience for the quick and systematic conduct of the business. An
immense stock of furniture and carpets is carried, embracing all styles, from
the plainest to the handsomest, and which, being bought direct, are placed to
the public at most reasonable prices. Mr. Schmitz is a gentleman well known
in and out of business circles, and has built up his business in the face of the
keenest competition. His prices will compare favorably with any other house
in the State, and parties here and elsewhere will find it to their advantage to
call on him. He also makes a specialty of manufacturing mattresses and
spring bottoms; his work in this respect being equal to any in the country.
The trade will do well to note this last addition, and to write Mr. Schmitz for
particulars.

THE TEXAS ABSTRACT COMPANY—Jas. A. Dickenson, President,
      James P. Crane, Secretary; Principal Office, 921 Congress Avenue,
      Austin, Texas.

The immense increase of the population of Texas within the past few
years, and the consequent proportionate increase in the value of lands has led
to many vexatious lawsuits, which, with proper care and consulting competent
parties, would have been avoided. The "Texas Abstract Company," has for
its object the perfecting of titles, which, through carelessness, and other causes,
have become imperfect; and with this view, they have prepared the most complete series of abstracts in the State, comprising abstracts not only from
Travis and all organized counties, but, also from all the unorganized counties
in the State. They also deal largely in Real Estate, make loans to any
amount, pay taxes for non-residents on land in any part of the State,

and are general agents for claims against the State. The officers are James A. Dickenson, President, and James P. Crane, Secretary; both gentlemen are well known, and of long and thorough experience in their business. Possessing ample facilities and connections, they invite correspondence. in all matters pertaining to their business. Any information is promptly given, and parties here and elsewhere having transactions in their line, will find it to their advantage to call on or correspond with them. A prominent fact connected with this company, and one which the public will do well to bear in mind, is, that this is the *only company in the State of Texas doing a general abstract business.*

W. B. SWEENY—Real Estate and Rental Agent; 714 Congress Avenue.

This gentleman can be found at his office at No. 714 Congress Avenue, where for the past 14 years he has conducted a financial, real estate and rental agency. His qualifications are such as to adapt him to this special line of business. His well-known integrity, ability and extensive experience have won him a patronage that is as lasting as it is merited. Besides selling and renting of city property, he also handles country property, such as farms and improved lands. He is courteous and affable to all his patrons, and, as a result, they are pleased with their business relations. In the insurance business, which is a part of his enterprise, he has associated with him Mr. C. F. Hill, an active young man, and with the experience of age and the activity of youth, the future success of this department is assured. They represent some of the most prominent insurance companies in the country, both fire and life, and can place policies in companies they feel assured are absolutely safe. All business transactions with this firm, we are confident, will prove pleasant, and be as represented.

W. H. FIREBAUGH & CO.—Dealers in Hardware, and Plow and Wagon Materials ; 212 and 214 Pecan Street.

Among the firms in this city engaged in the hardware business, W. H. Firebaugh & Co. occupy a prominent place, both by reason of the energy and enterprise which characterize their transactions, and the magnitude of their operations. The buildings occupied are conveniently located and well arranged for the business for which they are used. The main building is a two story structure, covering an area of 46x120 feet, and the warehouse adjoining is a one story building, 46x120 feet in size. This gives an immense amount of room, but no more than is needed to accommodate the large stock carried. This stock consists of a full line of shelf and heavy hardware, cutlery, plow and wagon materials, barb wire, tinware, belting, etc. This firm buy their goods in large quantities, thus getting the benefit of the lowest prices, and this, together with their facilities for handling goods cheaply, enables them to offer their customers inducements in the way of cheap goods, that other firms find it hard to compete with. In consequence they have a large trade, extending over a great part of the surrounding country, and aggregating more than $100,000 annually. The *personnel* of the firm is composed of W. H. Firebaugh, G. W. Bartholomew, and C. W. Firebaugh, all gentlemen of high standing among the business men of the community, and who possess the confidence of their friends and patrons. They pay the strictest personal attention to their business, conducting it upon principles of the most progressive enterprise and the broadest liberality, and the large permanent patronage which they enjoy and the rapid increase of their business speak volumes for the popularity of their house. We cheerfully recommend Messrs. W. H. Firebaugh & Co. to the confidence and patronage of our readers, feeling assured that any business relations which may be established with them will be found both pleasant and profitable.

CAPITAL BUSINESS COLLEGE AND SCHOOL OF PENMANSHIP, SHORTHAND, TYPE-WRITING AND TELEGRAPHY—923 CONGRESS AVENUE.

J. J. Anderson, A. M., President, Teacher of Mathematics, Science of Wealth, German, etc.; D. A. Griffits, M. A., Secretary, Teacher of Theory and Practice of Book-keeping, Business and Ornamental Penmanship, etc.; T. J. Ray, Teacher of the Spanish Language and Literature; Thomas Murray, Teacher of Shorthand and Type-writing; B. Morrall, Teacher of Telegraphy; A. H. Graham, Lecturer on Commercial Law; C. E. Roth, Instructor in Physical Education.

Among the most important institutions not only of Texas, but of the South, is the Capital Business College, whose name heads our article. Its establishment has filled a long-felt want, enabling our young men to obtain a THOROUGH business education without the enormous expense incident to a course at the Northern and Eastern business colleges. The location of the college is all that can be desired, being on the busiest thoroughfare of the city, and commanding a fine view from the twenty-four windows which give it light and air. , It is admirably furnished with all modern conveniences and appliances. Since its opening in 1882, two hundred and fifty students from all parts of the Union, even from Europe, have been enrolled on its books. Professor Anderson is an educator of long and varied experience, holding the position of Vice-President of the National Agricultural Association, and is also a contributor to several leading periodicals of the day, among which are the New York Agriculturalist, Texas Farm and Ranche, Texas Siftings, San Antonio Express, and others; and he is also now preparing for publication the first

number of " Men and Money," a work devoted to financial interests and business education. His corps of assistants are equally efficient in their respective
departments. The general and special rates of tuition are as follows:

Life Scholarship, which entitles the holder to Instruction in
    Book-keeping, Arithmetic, Penmanship, Grammar, Rhetoric
    and Political Economy, Commercial Law, Spelling, Reading
    and Letter-writing, allowing a year or more of study to be
    taken at one time or different times...................... $60.00
The same course limited to six months..................... 50.00
The same course limited to three months.................. 45.00
A course in Business and Ornamental Penmanship.......... 25.00
Course in Telegraphy, with privilege of attending the Penman-
    ship Class daily....................................... 30.00
Spanish, per month, night sessions........................ 2.50
German, per month, night sessions........................ 2.50

Special arrangements will be made with students of Phonography, Type-
writing, Physical Education and evening classes. Tuition in all departments
paid in advance unless special arrangements are made.

CLUB RATES.

When two pupils from the same family, or from the same neighborhood,
take scholarships at the same time, there is a deduction of ten per cent; when
three enter together, fifteen per cent is discounted; and when four or more,
twenty per cent is deducted from cost of scholarship as given above. Board
and lodging cost students from $15 to $20 per month.

There are no vacations in the Capital Business College. Students are
admitted at all times and without examination or special qualifications.
Students not well prepared get a thorough preparatory training here. The
College Literary Society offers students excellent opportunities for improvement in Debates, Extempore Addresses, Declamations, and Writing Essays;
and business men and firms in need of book-keepers and salesmen will consult their interest by opening correspondence with the Capital Business
College.

ZERR & BUASS—Galvanized Iron Cornices and Metal Roofing; Near
    Congress Avenue.

This is probably the only firm in the city engaged in this line of business,
and the business carried on is of such importance, that our work would be
incomplete were we to omit it. They manufacture galvanized iron cornices
and metal roofing, and on most of our finest buildings can be seen a specimen
of their work. Their trade is not only located in Austin, but extends over the

surrounding country, and they are constantly receiving orders from different sections of the State for work of this kind. Their prices are very reasonable, and all work is guaranteed to give perfect satisfaction. Employment is given to seven skilled workmen, all of whom are experienced hands, and the proprietors give their personal attention to all work done. They are located near Congress Avenue, and the building occupied has all the facilities for carrying on a business of this description. Messrs. M. Zerr & J. O. Buass, compose the firm. They are both experienced in this business, having thoroughly learned the trade, and we commend them to the public, feeling assured that all work done by them will give perfect satisfaction. Our many readers throughout the State who are in need of work of this kind will consult their own interests by corresponding with this firm before placing their work elsewhere.

F. EVERETT—Real Estate Agent and Notary Public; 812 Congress Avenue.

Among the numerous enterprises carried on in this busy hive of industry, and which by no means should be omitted in a work of this description, are the real estate interests, contributing, as they do, largely to the wealth and prosperity of the city. Among those firms engaged in this useful branch of trade, who have won a name for activity and thorough business ability, is the house of F. Everett, located at 812 Congress Avenue. He conducts principally a notary public business, and deeds, mortgages and legal business papers receive his personal attention. He has for a number of years been identified with the real estate business in this city, and his extended acquaintance with valuable property in different portions of the city and State, makes him a most desirable person to consult by those contemplating investment. His transactions are all conducted upon fair and honorable business principles, making his services almost invaluable to those requiring the aid of a real estate agent. Mr. Everett's prompt and straightforward manner has won for him the confidence and esteem of the entire community. To our many readers scattered over the North and West we recommend this house, feeling assured that all business entrusted to his care will be most satisfactorily transacted.

D. W. JONES & CO.—Furniture and Carpets; 805 and 807 Congress Avenue.

Among the most prominent of the business houses which line Congress Avenue is the firm of D. W. Jones & Co. They occupy a commodious building, 50x160 feet in dimensions, and two stories in height, besides having ample room for outside storage. The building is fitted out with every convenience for the prompt and systematic conduct of the business, ten hands being kept constantly busy filling the orders which come from city as well as country buyers. The stock averages $50,000 in value, and consists of as complete a line of furniture, carpets and upholstery goods as can be found in any city in the country. Here are seen all styles of furniture, from the neatest and plainest cottage sets, to the most expensive and elegant products of the leading factories. Carpets of all hues and designs, English and American, and upholstery goods of every description. These being bought direct, are placed to the trade at manufacturers' prices, and the large and fast-increasing trade of this well-known house, is evidence of the superior quality of their goods and their reasonable terms. All goods sold by this firm have a reputation for quality, a fact which is now a source of great pride to Mr. John C. Boak, who is now the sole member of the firm. Mr. Boak is well known in and out of business circles, and, with the rapid growth of Austin, there is no limit to the future extension of his business.

R. H. KIRBY—Land and General Agent; No. 816 Congress Avenue.

Austin has several prominent land agents, and most are conducting a general land business on commission. The business conducted by the subject of this sketch is more in buying for cash when decided bargains are offered, and thus providing himself with land that he can offer decided advantages on, when capitalists call upon him to make paying investments. He has been in Austin eight years, and for about two years has been conducting this business. He is a prompt operator, and always has on his books a large list of property that selections can be made from, which will prove valuable investments. Parties who are compelled to realize on their lands will find, by corresponding with Mr. Kirby, an outlet from their embarrassments, and at fair and honorable rates. We can commend him to our patrons as a desirable man to consult on land matters.

STACY & HICKS—Jobbers of Cigars and Tobacco; 106 West Pecan Street.

In compiling a historical work such as this, embracing a review of the most prominent houses engaged in the different branches of commercial pursuits, we find establishments here and there, which deserve somewhat more than a passing notice at our hands, by reason of the immense amount of business done, the large degree of popularity which they enjoy, and the spirit of enterprise, activity and progressiveness which pervades their every department and promotes their every transaction. Such an establishment is the one presided over by the well-known and no less popular firm of Stacy & Hicks, at 106 West Pecan Street. This firm have been doing business here for nearly a year, and have already become known throughout the entire West as being one of the most honorable and reliable houses to deal with. The building

used is commodious, and is fitted up in such a manner as to make this establishment one of the most complete in the State, in point of equipments and
for convenience and facility in handling goods. These gentlemen are dealers
in tobaccos and cigars, and keep all the desirable brands of the day. They
are sole agents for the Star Route, Mardi Gras, and numerous other cigars, and
for the Piper Heidsiech chewing tobacco, which is known throughout the
United States for its delicious champagne flavor. The trade of this house is
so extensive that it is necessary to keep two traveling salesmen on the road
continually. The individual members of the firm are Wm. H. Stacy and
Chas. T. Hicks, the former having been a resident of Austin for the past
eleven years, and the latter five years; and it can be truthfully stated that
they have won the esteem and respect of the community, by their upright,
honorable course, courteous manners and fair dealings. Their business policy
is prompt and liberal, and we cordially commend them to our many readers
throughout the West, as being a firm that offer superior advantages to dealers
in this line of goods, and correspondence with the house will undoubtedly
open up business transactions both profitable and pleasant.

CAPITAL OIL COMPANY—C. W. Hopkins, Manager; 106 West Pecan
    Street.

Since the establishment of this company three years ago, with its perfect
system of delivery of oil, the citizens of Austin surely have had no reason
to complain. The company having sold only high-test and superior oil that
could be relied upon, and given full measure, as well as delivered it at their
residences free of cost, and at any time and in any quantity as might be
desired. Mr. Hopkins' office is with Messrs. Stacy & Hicks, where all orders
can be left, and they will receive the earliest attention and prompt delivery.
We are glad to know that housekeepers are generally favoring this enterprise,
as they find thereby that their groceries are free from any oil odor, as was formerly the case when delivered with their groceries. Doing an extensive
business and making it a specialty, he is enabled to buy in larger lots, thus
making a saving in purchase, which profit he divides with his patrons. The
enterprise is a credit to the city, and should receive very liberal patronage.

A. GARDNER & CO.—Lumber Dealers and Planing Mill; Congress
    Avenue.

This new and enterprising establishment is favorably located near Congress Avenue, and has large yard room to handle the stock of lumber, laths,
shingles, and stock usually found in a first-class lumber yard. In connection,
also, they have a new planing mill, sash, door and blind factory, with ample
steam power, and all the most modern improved machinery to conduct the

same. All building material is here prepared at short notice, and can be relied on as being finished in a perfect and superior manner. None but skilled men are given employment here, and good work is required at their hands. Parties who desire business in their line, whether merchants or builders, will find them a liberal and progressive firm, and one which takes good care of their patrons. With the best facilities to supply themselves with lumber, they can compete with any similar concern in the State in selling lumber at low prices. Being manufacturers of builders' material, they can deal with the closest buyers. In advantages offered to the trade, both in quality and price of goods, the firm compete successfully with any, and as a desirable one with which to establish agreeable, profitable and permanent relations, has no superior anywhere.

EDWARD W. SHANDS & SON — GENERAL REAL ESTATE AND INSURANCE; 163 EAST PECAN STREET.

In reviewing the industries of Austin, we find some that are entitled to prominent notice on account of the length of time they have been in business, as well as the honorable conduct that has been manifested in all their transactions. Among these is the firm of Shands & Son. The elder, formerly in this business in St. Louis, came to Austin while it was an infant city, and by his familiarity with the rise and value of the property of the city, is well qualified to handle intelligently any interests entrusted to his charge. Lately he has had the assistance of his son, who, as a partner, is an invaluable help in prosecuting the business successfully. Both the real estate and insurance departments are efficiently managed and honorably conducted, and it is with no small degree of pleasure we make notice of this firm in reviewing the history of Austin, as we can assure our readers they are well worthy of confidence.

WAYLAND & CRISER—WHOLESALE AND RETAIL GROCERS; 807 CONGRESS AVENUE.

Among the business houses which line Congress Avenue, one of the largest and best known is that of Messrs. Wayland & Criser, whose name heads our article. Their building is a substantial and commodious one, and is fitted out with every convenience for the quick and systematic conduct of the business. Their stock comprises all that can be found in an essentially first-class grocery establishment, and is constantly replenished; care being taken to keep up with the latest novelties in all departments. The trade, which reaches a large and rapidly increasing amount, extends throughout the city and State; the superior quality of their groceries finding favor wherever they are introduced. Transacting a large wholesale as well as retail business, all their goods are bought direct; hence, they are enabled to place them to the

trade, as well as to consumers, at terms which few can duplicate. Messrs.
Wayland & Criser are both gentlemen well known in and out of business circles, and have built up their present fine business in the face of the keenest
competition. Messrs. Wayland & Criser also do a large commission and produce business, receiving consignments of butter, fruits and other produce, and
watching closely the markets, they are enabled to procure the very best prices
for consignments. They also possess ample storage facilities for any amount
of produce. Under their favorable auspices, and with the rapid growth of
Austin, there is no limit to the future extension of their business. All communications receive prompt attention, and parties here and elsewhere will find
it to their advantage to call on or correspond with them.

O. N. HOLLINGSWORTH—LAND AND LIVE STOCK AGENCY; 717 CONGRESS
AVENUE, AUSTIN, TEXAS.

Although not long established, the transactions of the above firm will
compare favorably with those of any similar one in Austin. Mr. Hollingsworth has on his books large tracts of the best grazing lands scattered throughout Texas, Old and New Mexico, and which he offers at most reasonable terms,
so as to place a comfortable home within the reach of all. Besides these large
surveys, he has in different sections of the State, small surveys adapted either
to grazing or farming, and also in Travis and adjacent counties he has improved farms for sale. He has also a number of desirable city residences and
lots for sale. But it is of the splendid ranche at Fort Stockton that we desire
especially to speak. The ranche comprises an area of 42,000 acres; 6,000
acres of which can be irrigated immediately, the ditches being cut, and the
water ready to be turned on. On these lands 25 to 30 bushels of wheat, and
35 to 40 bushels of corn per acre can be easily grown. The Frijola Bean
grows luxuriantly; the celebrated El Paso and other grapes flourish and fruits
of all kinds and garden vegetables can be raised in large quantities. The
adjacent country is thickly set with the nutritious Gamma Grass which
matures in the early Fall into natural hay. Upwards of 1,000,000 acres
are directly tributary to and are drained by the beautiful stream which irri-
gates the valley of this magnificent ranche. Being at an altitude of about
3,000 feet above the sea, the air is singularly pure; hence the cattle raised
here are free from all character of disease. At present three hundred head of
horses, and thirteen thousand cattle range here, each year showing a great
increase of their number; and so fine is the climate, and so rich the pasture,
that six times that number could easily be maintained. Besides this, there is
a United States Fort with garrison, officers' quarters, and immense and thoroughly fitted out stables which could be utilized for housing and properly
caring for improved stock. With all these combined advantages, Fort Stock-

ton Ranche could be made the finest breeding farm in the world, and the point to which stockraisers in various parts of the country would send to procure their choicest breeding animals. This splendid property, which includes the Fort and about thirty other houses, is now for sale, and we commend the above sketch to the careful consideration of those who would make a safe and profitable investment. All communications addressed to Mr. Hollingsworth regarding this or any other property which he has for sale, will receive prompt attention.

MORRISON & FOURMY—DIRECTORY PUBLISHERS. ESTABLISHED 1876. MAIN OFFICE, 170 TREMONT STREET, GALVESTON.

In no branch of the publishing business has there been greater progress made in the last score of years, than in that devoted to the publishing of city directories. Prior to the civil war it was only the very large cities of the country that boasted a directory, and even those few were insignificant publications, compared with those of to-day, being too feebly supported by the business public to justify a publishing house in expending the time, labor and capital requisite to make them the comprehensive *vademecums* they should have been and are now. But the enterprising publishers of America have been indefatigable in their efforts to educate the masses up to a full knowledge of the indispensable value of a thoroughly complete and reliable city directory, and as a result, we now find that the most ordinary towns in every section of our country clamor each year for a new directory, and it is a slow-poke community indeed that will not contribute liberally to the publishing of a new directory of their town at least once every two years. No publishing firm has done more to bring about this improved condition of intelligence, than Messrs. Morrison & Fourmy, the well-known publishers of Texas City Directories (established in 1876), and too much credit cannot be accorded them for the good they have accomplished, the benefits they are continually conferring upon the public at large and the important influence they are exerting upon the development of our cities and towns throughout the State through their invaluable directories. The firm now publishes regularly, annual or bi-ennial directories, in the cities of Galveston, Houston, San Antonio, Dallas, Austin, Waco, Fort Worth, Sherman and Dennison—all live, go-ahead Texas cities—and also Shreveport, Louisiana. The rapid advances which these several cities are making as centers of trade, commerce and industry; must in a very considerable measure be ascribed to such valuable adjuncts as the well-printed, comprehensive and thoroughly reliable directory they each support liberally and with the spirit of true nineteenth century progression. The main office of this extensive directory publishing house is located at No. 170 Tremont street, Galveston, and where are kept on file all directories of the principal cities of the United

States, and also back files of their own Texas publications, for reference, free to
the general public. Messrs. Morrison & Fourmy are arranging to add several
other live Texas cities to their list of directory publications this year, another
evidence of the appreciation by the public of their capable works.

F. E. RUFFINI—Architect, over Samostz' Drug Store; Congress Avenue.

The art of architecture, which in ancient times assumed grand proportions, during the present century has made rapid strides toward perfection, and
at the present time for variety and beauty of style, for durability, strength
and pleasing appearance it seems to have reached its acme. These thoughts

have come to us while viewing
some of the structures built under
the masterly plans of Mr. F. E.
Ruffini, an artist who has reached
the top round of the profession,
as is evidenced by the patronage
he is receiving from the public
where he resides; and he is well
worthy of the confidence of our
readers abroad who desire the
services of a competent architect.
Not only do many of the public buildings of Austin stand as a monument to
his skill, but the beauty and convenience of many of our most admired residences show evidences of his masterly work. Parties throughout the State can
reach him by correspondence and will receive prompt replies. We are glad to
add that he is considered in Austin not only a man of ability, but conscientious
and reliable in all business transactions. He employs skilled help and guarantees all work to give perfect satisfaction. He provides competent men to
superintend his plans in building when desired, and he is recognized among
the profession as being one of the first. His terms are as liberal as can be had
where the same ability is desired.

PAUL PRESSLER—Sole Agent for Semps' St. Louis Lager Beer; Office and Beer Vaults, N. E. Corner Cypress and Guadalupe Streets opposite I. & G. N. R. R. Freight Depot.

The qualities for which Semps' St. Louis Lager Beer is noted are chiefly
distinguisded for purity, brilliancy of color, richness of flavor and non-liability,
to deteriorate in warm climates—qualities, the result of excellent water, coupled
with the use of apparatus possessing all the best modern improvements and the
superior standard of both quality and quantity of ingredients used, all of which
has resulted in producing a beer which for palatableness, flavor, tonic qualities

is not surpassed anywhere and has made the beer famous and giving it a world-wide reputation and increasing demand. Mr. Paul Pressler, sole agent for this beer, has been connected with it since its first introduction to Austin and has managed the business with that admirable tact and ability acquired by long experience in the beering trade. He is a popular man and has already brought up the annual sales of this beer to about 100 carloads. He has provided all facilities to keep the beer in an even temperature so that when ordered it is sent out in a fresh and healthy state. Our readers from abroad who may desire to handle a beer that is strictly first-class should not fail to correspond with Mr. Pressler, who will be prompt and faithful to his patrons. The office and beer vaults are located directly opposite the freight depot of the International & Great Northern Railroad, thus affording him advantages in receiving and shipping beer, the importance of which is apparent.

LAND & THOMPSON—REAL ESTATE AND LAND AGENCY, FOR THE SALE, PURCHASE, EXCHANGE AND LEASE OF IMPROVED AND UNIMPROVED PROPERTY; ALSO, FIRE INSURANCE AGENTS; DALLAS, TEXAS.

The importance of the commission agent in the business affairs of this life is thoroughly understood by every intelligent, wide-awake man of the nineteenth century. No other medium is so capable for establishing the most intimate relations between the seller and the buyer—no matter how utter strangers all parties may be or how widely separated by distance—and no other medium labors so assiduously to promote their respective interests by conferring upon either party alike special advantages and otherwise unattainable benefits. He is the mutual friend and adviser, or go-between, that may be relied upon implicitly, and in no branch of business has his services been sought to a greater extent, and with more gratifying results, than in matters pertaining to real estate. The firm of Land & Thompson, Dallas, Texas, are one of the many engaged in this occupation that can be commended to the public at large as *eminently qualified* and *thoroughly reliable*, having been closely connected with the business for the past twenty years. Their experience, comprehensive knowledge of the real estate and land business in every detail, and extensive facilities for safely conducting it in all its various branches, together with their wide acquaintance with capitalists, large land operators, manufacturers and others interested in land properties, gives them very decided advantages over the majority of Texas land agents, and enables the firm to guarantee the most perfect satisfaction in the transacting of all business entrusted to their charge. They buy, sell, exchange, lease and rent farms, ranches, and improved or unimproved lands of all descriptions. They pay taxes on property and keep up improvements and insurance policies. They make a specialty of looking after non-resident property owners interests, with the same watchful care they exercise over their own property, and invite correspondence from either holders of Texas property, at home or abroad, on the subject of this department of their business. They are also prepared to locate scrip on choice lands, perfect titles, value lands, make divisions of property, make loans on choice farms or valuable lands of any description, and make investments for capitalists. In their department devoted to city business they give the same careful and experienced attention to buying and selling or exchange of real estate, renting and collection of rents, keeping property in repair, insuring, paying of taxes, the general care of estates belonging to residents or non-residents. The firm also places fire risks upon all classes of portable property and improved real estate in the staunchest insurance companies in the country. In this connection they are prepared to represent any fire insurance company of merit that desires to enter the State of Texas, and will entertain proposals from corporations to that end. The firm make a leading specialty of handling lands suitable for agriculture and stock purposes, and invite the *particular* attention of stockmen and farmers to their extensive facilities and superior inducements. They control over *one million acres* of the finest farming and grazing lands in the State, and which they are now placing on the market, to be sold at unusually low rates to *actual settlers*. Messrs. Land and Tnompson are capable, energetic business men, of firm integrity, sound judgment, and conservative management, possessed of unquestionable executive ability and financial talents of a high order, who are liberally endorsed by the best citizens of Texas and the South, as well as of the Western and Eastern cities. Enterprising, skillful operators, keeping fully abreast with the progressive age, and possessing a complete knowledge of the magnificent resources of Texas for agriculture, stock-raising, mining, manufactures, commerce and capital, and moreover laboring with a keen interest in the development of that grand destiny which every penetrative mind recognizes as the future portion of the State, the firm of Land & Thompson commends *itself* to the public as one from whom the most liberal treatment may be expected, and who may be relied upon to the fullest extent for the judicious handling of all interests placed in their charge, and with the highest possible advantages to their patrons.

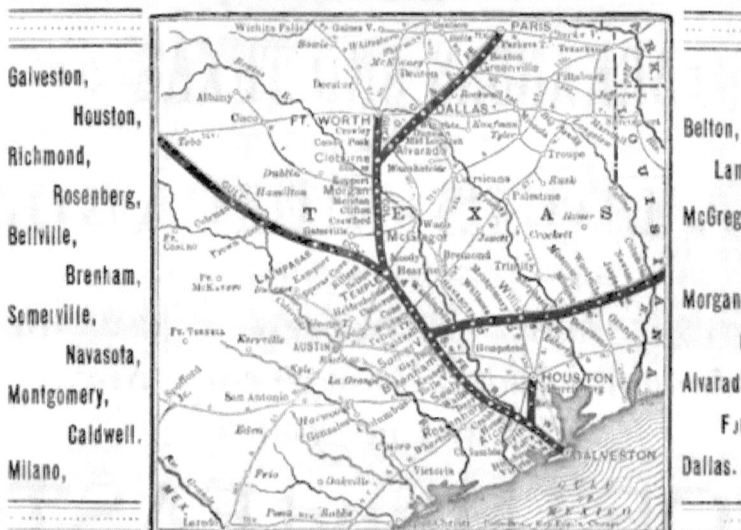

A Two Cent Stamp

Sent with your full address to A. V. H. CARPENTER, General Passenger Agent, Milwaukee, Wis., will bring to you one of the following named publications, issued for free distribution by the

Chicago, Milwaukee & St. Paul Railway.

If you desire to know where to spend the Summer, ask for a "GUIDE TO SUMMER HOMES" and a copy of "GEMS OF THE NORTHWEST." If you think of going to

Omaha,	San Francisco,
Denver,	St. Paul,
Minneapolis, etc.	

ask for "A TALE OF NINE CITIES." If you want to invest in, or go to, any portion of the Western States or Territories, ask for a copy of our 28-page illustrated pamphlet, entitled, "THE NORTHWEST AND FAR WEST." All of these publications contain valuable information, which can be obtained in no other way.